F
LEV   Levinson, ...yn

           And don't bring
           Jeremy

DATE DUE

And Don't Bring Jeremy

And Don't Bring Jeremy

Marilyn Levinson

Illustrated by Diane de Groat

Henry Holt and Company

New York

Published by Henry Holt and Company, Inc.,
521 Fifth Avenue, New York, New York 10175.
Distributed in Canada by Fitzhenry & Whiteside Limited,
195 Allstate Parkway, Markham, Ontario L3R 4T8.

Library of Congress Cataloging in Publication Data
Levinson, Marilyn.
And don't bring Jeremy.
Summary: New in the neighborhood and eager to be
part of a new crowd, sixth-grader Adam finds it
difficult to come to terms with the needs of his
older brother who suffers from a learning disability
and often seems younger himself.
    1. Children's stories, American. [1. Brothers—
Fiction.   2. Learning disabilities—Fiction.
3. Friendship—Fiction.   4. Baseball—Fiction]
I. De Groat, Diane, ill.   II. Title.
PZ7.L5793An   1985   [Fic]   84-22484
ISBN: 0-8050-0554-4

Designer: Victoria Hartman
Printed in the United States of America
10 9 8 7 6 5 4 3 2

ISBN 0-8050-0554-4

To my sons, David and Michael
And to Roberta Gellis . . . writer, teacher, and friend

CHAPTER

1

"**C**ome on, Adam. Throw another fastball. Right over the plate."

For the eightieth time that afternoon I stared at Eddie Gordon, trying to figure out why he was suddenly acting so friendly and nice. Eddie was in seventh grade, a year ahead of me, and the best player on our Little League team. He was lots of fun to be with, someone I'd hoped to have as a friend, but up until a few days ago he'd always acted as if he didn't even know I existed.

His small, wiry frame crouched behind home plate. He shook his head of kinky red hair that reminded me of Raggedy Andy—not that I'd ever tell him so. "Come on," he shouted impatiently. "What are you waiting for?"

That was more like him. Eddie was generous, but, boy, could he fly off the handle. Winding up, I forgot about Eddie and concentrated on his outstretched mitt. I pictured the batter standing before him, fixing where his knees and shoulders should be. I let the ball go. It smacked into the waiting mitt.

"Strike!" Eddie called. "That's the sixth in a row," he

added, grinning as though he'd thrown them himself.

I nodded and held back my grin. I'd been in enough neighborhood ball games with Eddie in these few months since we'd moved to Glen Haven to know better than to let him see me get excited. He'd only make fun and tell me to stop showing off, like I'd seen him do to other kids. Or worse, he'd think I was trying to take over his position as starting pitcher on our baseball team.

"Go for another strike," Eddie yelled, tossing the ball back to me.

I wound up and threw another fastball.

"Another one! Jeez. Dad better let you pitch tomorrow. Just keep this up and we'll cream those Lawson Cleaners."

I refused to get carried away by Eddie's enthusiasm. He had a habit of building things up and getting real upset when they didn't work out.

"That'll be pretty hard to do. They won two out of two games so far," I reminded him. "I hear they have great hitters and fantastic fielding." I glanced away, to the low brick elementary school I'd been attending for the last three months, hoping I hadn't gone too far.

"Yeah, well let me tell you something," Eddie said, sauntering over to me. "My father said last night that with you and me pitching, Mark and Danny on second and third, and Richie catching, we have a good chance of winning tomorrow."

So I definitely was going to pitch in tomorrow's game! Fantastic! Although pitchers in our division were allowed to pitch all six innings, Mr. Gordon liked using two pitchers, for three innings each. Last week he'd let me pitch during the last inning, after Jeff walked three men in a row. I did pretty well, too, giving up a walk, then striking out two men. But I decided to play it modest.

"Won't your father put Jeff in to pitch ahead of me? I mean, he's in seventh grade."

Eddie shrugged his shoulders. "He'll pitch, too, I guess. But Dad thinks you're better."

I couldn't help grinning. "We sure did great last week, with your home run and Mark's double."

"Yeah, and we would have won the first game, too, if Jeremy hadn't thrown that ball wild to third base instead of home."

I bit my lip. Eddie's voice turned mean when he mentioned my brother.

"Yeah, well," I began, not knowing what I was about to say. That Jeremy had even gotten his hands on the ball was pretty amazing. "I guess it wasn't too smart."

I squirmed and looked down at my sneakers. The right laces were untied. I kneeled down to tie them, feeling my face turn red.

"Why did Jeremy bother to sign up for Little League?" Eddie persisted. "He couldn't care less about baseball. All he does is take up space in the outfield."

Here I was again, having to explain Jeremy. "My mom thought it would be good for him," I mumbled. I didn't want to get up and see Eddie's freckled face, which turned as red as his hair when he got angry, but I felt foolish hunched over my sneaker. Forget it. I stood up. I mean, I wasn't responsible for Jeremy, was I?

"Yeah, well, he isn't doing our team any good. He never even gets a walk because he swings at every ball they throw him, without coming within ten feet of touching it."

Eddie must have seen me wince because suddenly he was apologizing. "Sorry, Adam," he said gruffly. "It's not *your* fault."

I shrugged but Eddie could see that I was hurt.

"At least one member of the Krasner family is a great baseball player," he said. "Get your bat and hit a few. Too bad Mark and Danny couldn't make it today."

I was sorry, too. Mark was in seventh grade like Eddie and Jeremy. His cousin Danny Martin was in my class. They were both nice kids, always laughing and clowning around without going too far. And they never made jokes about Jeremy like Eddie sometimes did—not that I blamed him at times. Jeremy was hard to take.

I reached for the new metal bat Dad bought me the week before and stood ready. Eddie wound up, then stared at something in the parking lot behind me. He dropped the ball.

"Oh, no," he said, disgusted. "Look who's coming."

I turned and saw Jeremy loping toward us, his head down as usual. He was the last person I wanted to see right then. He stopped in front of me, panting.

"Mom wants you home now. Your orthodontist appointment's in half an hour. 'Lo, Eddie."

Eddie barely lifted his hand, not bothering to hide his dislike.

I'd forgotten all about the appointment, but for some reason or other I just stood there. I didn't feel like running home just because Jeremy said I should.

"Come on," he scolded. "Mom said to hurry."

"In a minute," I snapped. "Go on home. I'll be right there."

Jeremy looked uncertain, as he always did when I yelled at him. It made me sorry that I had. After all, he *was* older. And he was never mean or nasty. Only annoying and immature—and not really good at anything.

I put my hand on his arm. "Go on, I'll be right there."

I smiled and he smiled back. Then he turned around and took off in his funny way—half-running, half-walking, as though he were limping. I felt bad for him, sticking out like a sore thumb in everything he did. All because of something that went wrong when he was born. But I felt bad for me, too—always afraid the other kids wouldn't want to be friendly with me once they found out I was Jeremy's brother.

I reached down for my mitt. "Guess I better go. See you tomorrow. At the game."

"I better get going, too," Eddie said, probably not wanting to be the only one left. "In case Dad comes home from work early. He's taking me to buy a new mitt."

"That's great," I said. I hooked my mitt onto the handlebars of my bicycle, then lay the bat across. "See you at the field. One-fifteen, right?" I kicked up the kickstand, ready to go.

"Adam?"

I turned around to see what Eddie wanted.

"We—Mark and Danny and me—well, we were thinking of going out for pizza before the game tomorrow. At Gino's. Want to come?"

"Sure, why not? I'll check with my mom and let you know." I shrugged my shoulders, trying to shake the uneasy feeling that just took hold of me. What was wrong?

"Great. Meet us there at twelve. Bring your bicycle. Then we'll ride over to the field early and practice before the rest of the team comes."

I suddenly knew. "All right." In spite of myself, Mom's drilling me to try to include Jeremy whenever I could won out. "But is it all right if I—"

"And Adam—" His voice cut across my question.

"Hm?"

"And don't bring Jeremy. Okay?"

CHAPTER

2

"Why can't I go, too?" Jeremy asked. As usual he was chewing with his lips open so I had to see his mashed-up chicken. It was disgusting.

"Ick," I said. "Close your mouth when you eat. I told you, you weren't invited."

"But I'm on the team." He started to whine. "They should have invited me, too."

Thank God Dad took over. "Look, Jeremy, we've been through this before. We go someplace only when we've been invited to go. You know that."

Jeremy sniffed and ate his chicken. I took a bite of mine. No one said a word.

"Adam," my mother said two minutes later, "you're not eating your squash."

I knew she'd say something. Anything. Mom couldn't stand silence at the dinner table—thought it was unnatural. Also, she was probably annoyed with me for not bringing Jeremy along for lunch tomorrow.

"I know," I answered. "I don't like squash."

"But you said you'd try it tonight."

"Only because you nagged."

"That's enough, Adam," Dad said sternly.

"Sorry, Dad, but she knows I hate squash."

"I want to go for pizza, too," Jeremy said loudly. "Adam always gets to go to parties and sleepovers and I don't. It isn't fair."

Mom lost her patience. "For goodness sake, Adam, couldn't he go along? It would be easier for me. I have so much to do tomorrow."

"Sorry, Mom. I can't." To keep the peace, I didn't bother to add that I was specifically asked not to bring him, and boy, was I glad.

Mom just sighed and looked knowingly at me. In spite of her irritation she really understood. I only wished that the subject of going to Gino's for lunch had never come up. Eddie had called before dinner to see if I was coming. Of course, Mom and Jeremy *had* to be in the kitchen then and overheard my part of the conversation. Anyway, I did have to check it out with her, so I guess there was no way of avoiding this flak after all.

"Why do you want to go out with that Eddie Gordon anyway?" Jeremy asked. "You always said he was a nasty creep and a sore loser."

"That was before I got to know him better."

"I bet it's 'cause his father's the coach and you want to make sure he lets you pitch every game." Jeremy smiled his crooked smile. It was moments like this that I recognized the truth: my brother had problems all right, but in some ways he sure wasn't dumb.

"Don't be stupid," I yelled. "He's been pretty nice to me lately. The first kid around here who has been, I might add. And he's friendly with Mark and Danny and I like them."

Dad pushed back his chair and stood up. "Come on,

Jeremy, let's get to work. We have to fertilize the ground if you want to have a garden this summer."

Jeremy's eyes lit up. "Great! I'll go and get the stuff from the garage."

"Don't forget the shovel."

"And tomorrow after the game we'll go to the nursery and get peppers and lettuce and tomatoes and squash and corn. Just like you promised."

He flew out of his seat and down the steps to the den and into the garage. Jeremy was funny. He got excited about gardening like I did about baseball.

Dad put his hand on my shoulder. "We'll have our catch in about an hour, okay?"

"Sure, Dad." That would give me time to read the baseball scores in the paper and watch part of the game on TV. I got up and brought my dish to the sink, something Jeremy forgot to do for a change.

"Adam, you hardly touched your dinner," Mom complained.

"I'll make it up tomorrow," I promised her.

. . .

It was fun going to Gino's for lunch. I'd only eaten there once—with Jeremy and my parents—during the winter, when we first moved into the house. The kids at school always talked about meeting at Gino's. They'd ride over on their bicycles and drink Cokes and play the arcade games or just hang around outside. I never went there again because nobody had ever asked me to—until yesterday, that is.

It was kind of dark inside and I had to squint to see anything. I felt stupid and hoped the other boys were there.

"Hey, Adam. Over here," Eddie called.

Relieved, I followed his voice to a booth in the back of the long, narrow room. I slid in next to him. Danny and Mark, both grinning, were sitting on the other side. They were all wearing their gray and green uniform, like I was, and they seemed glad to see me.

Eddie was in a great mood, talking about how we were sure to win today. He kept reaching over to pat one of us and calling us "buddy" or "mate." It was easy to see why all the kids liked him. I didn't say much, but it sure felt good to be included.

"We'd better decide what we want to order," Mark said, "before the crowd gets here." Mark was big all over—what Mom would call stocky and I'd consider fat—except that I liked Mark. Also, he was a good, all-around ball player. His weight sure didn't keep him from making plays or from stealing bases when he wanted to.

"Good thinking," Eddie agreed. "What's everyone having?"

We decided to order a pie and a half, so everyone could have three pieces, and four Cokes. Eddie and Mark went up to the front to put in our order and wait for the food, since the waitress only served in the restaurant section.

Danny smiled at me across the table. "Don't expect them back with the food for at least ten minutes," he said. He was almost as tall as his cousin, but thin, with dark hair and blue eyes. And he had a nice smile. He wasn't part of the group of boys in our class who hung around with the girls, but sometimes I'd catch a few of the girls looking at him, like they thought he was good-looking.

Neither of us said anything for a while. I guess we were both shy or something. Finally Danny spoke.

"Do you like to paint?" he asked me.

"You mean paint pictures or houses? I'm not too good at either one."

"I don't mean either," he said, then burst out laughing.

I didn't know what on earth he was laughing at, only that it wasn't at me. Then suddenly his laughing struck me funny and I started laughing, too. There we were, carrying on like a couple of hyenas, about what I couldn't say. Except that it seemed the most natural thing in the world to do.

"I'm not explaining myself too well, am I?" he asked when we calmed down. "What I'm talking about is painting the sets for the class play."

"Oh," I said, surprised. "But I really can't draw or anything."

"Don't worry," he said quickly. "You don't have to. I just need someone to help me paint the sets after I've finished drawing them."

"Oh," I said again, not knowing if I wanted to or not. Danny must have decided that I wasn't going to because he began to reassure me.

"It's not a lot of work and it's really fun. We'd be working together. Of course it would be nice if we could get a few more kids, but everyone I've asked is involved with the play or just not interested."

So that was it. He couldn't get anyone else to help him. I should have figured that was the only reason he was acting friendly all of a sudden. He didn't really want *me*. I got that familiar sick feeling in the bottom of my stomach when I thought about making friends here in Glen Haven. Danny must have read my thoughts.

"I was going to talk to you about it in school, but Eddie

said you'd be coming here today so I waited till now."

His blue eyes seemed to be begging me to say yes. I decided to give it a chance, since Mom kept urging me to. Not to let that bad feeling take over. Why shouldn't I help him paint the sets? I liked Danny and I sure didn't have anything else to do after school. And Mom would be pleased. She'd say I was finally "getting used to my new environment."

"I'll help you," I said.

"That's great!" Danny grinned. "I don't know what I would have done if you hadn't said yes. Hey, why don't you come over tomorrow and I'll show you the sketches I made?"

"Okay," I said, grinning back at him. I didn't want to get my hopes up, but I had the definite feeling that I'd just made another friend.

Happiness must have made me very hungry because I ate all of my pizza plus Danny's last piece. And I got another Coke.

"Hey, Adam, where are you putting it all?" Eddie teased.

Danny giggled. "Adam's eating so much he won't be able to run."

"Sure I will," I told him. "You'll see. I'll fly—if I ever get to hit the ball."

Everyone laughed good-naturedly at that. I hadn't been doing too much hitting so far.

"Well, as long as you don't fall asleep at shortstop," Mark said. "That would be a disaster."

"You know I wouldn't do that," I said, beaming at the three of them. It was nice being included after all these months.

We rode our bikes over to the baseball field, giving ourselves a good half hour before the rest of the team was supposed to arrive. Eddie and I took the lead while Mark and Danny trailed behind, arguing fiercely over who had a better record over the years—Pete Rose or Carl Yastrzemski.

"I really shouldn't be telling you this," Eddie said to me, "but I may as well, since it's so close to game time."

I looked at him, suddenly excited.

"Dad said you'd be starting pitcher today," Eddie said, staring straight ahead. I couldn't tell if he was mad or not and for once I didn't care.

"Yippee!" I shouted, forgetting to act cool.

Eddie smiled. "I think he wants to surprise you, but I couldn't help telling you. Don't let on that I told, okay?"

"Sure," I said, only too happy to agree. Starting pitcher! Too bad Dad had to work and couldn't watch the game. But Mom would be there.

At the field we tossed the ball around, then practiced catching pop flies and grounders. We took turns batting as Eddie and I pitched. My arm felt great. I was sure I could strike out all nine batters in the three innings I was allowed to pitch.

Eddie's father arrived, then the umpire, then Richie, Eric, and Jeff—all seventh graders—and the rest of the team, my age or a year younger. Mom must have come while we were warming up because I happened to look up and saw her talking to Danny's mother. I waved and she waved back, then she continued her conversation. I was glad to see her talking to Mrs. Martin. Mom worked at the bank all day and hardly knew anyone in the neighborhood yet.

"'Lo, Adam."

Jeremy stood in front of me like he was waiting for me to tell him what to do.

"Here, Adam!"

I reached out and caught the ball Mark had thrown to me. Jeremy still stood there.

"Come on, Adam. Throw the ball," Eddie shouted.

"Go on, move," I told Jeremy. Seeing him standing there like a fool, I wished he'd disappear. He had no business interfering with my game and my new friends.

"Where should I go?"

I looked around for a gap in the large circle we had formed. I saw one near Richie and pointed. "Go over there."

He stared at the spot for a moment, then shuffled over. I felt like wringing his neck. As usual he didn't know what to do. And he always came to me to find out. I was glad when Mr. Gordon finally called us over for positions and last-minute instructions. Why did Mom have to put us both on the same team? Didn't she ever stop and think about the effect having a brother like Jeremy had on me?

The first half of the game moved slowly. It was boring, actually. Mr. Gordon had Eddie pitch the first three innings, so I was really disappointed. I mean, didn't Eddie just tell me that his father planned to make me starting pitcher? Or was Eddie just saying that for some stupid reason? I couldn't figure it out.

I played shortstop and didn't get to field one ball. Jeremy was far back in the outfield, along with the fifth graders. Eddie began striking out the other side one by one. Big Bob, the Lawson Cleaners' starting pitcher, did the same. At least there was some excitement in the

third inning. With two outs, Eddie gave up a walk, a single, and another walk. Another guy singled and drove in a run. Finally, with all of us holding our breath, Eddie struck the third man out.

By the time I got to pitch in the fourth inning, the score was tied at one apiece. Mark had hit a homer in the bottom of the third inning with no one on base. I wasn't nervous when I got to the mound, just excited.

I was off to an excellent start, striking out the first two men. Then one of their big hitters bounced a hard ball in my direction. I fielded it to Eddie on first for the last out. Everyone clapped and cheered. Boy, did that feel great!

We picked up a run in the bottom of the fourth inning, and the other team came back strong, determined to score. Two men singled back to back, then a third hit a pop-up and we doubled up the man at second. Two outs. When I struck the next guy out, I walked off the mound with a sigh of relief. Three more outs and we had the game.

Only it didn't happen that way.

I did strike out the first man. Then walked the second. No big deal, I thought. But Big Bob, their strongest hitter, was up again at bat. He slammed the first ball I threw him over my head. The guy I walked was nearing second base. I turned and saw Jeremy waving his hands above his head like a crazy man.

"Go away, go away," he was shouting to the fifth graders running toward him. "I've got it. It's mine!"

He cupped his other hand to his mitt and the ball landed—right at his feet.

"Dammit, Jeremy," I shouted.

One of the other fielders picked up the ball to throw it

to Danny on third. But it was too late. Big Bob was reaching home plate.

"Who cares?" Jeremy said as he walked off the field. "It's only a game."

That did it! I jumped on his back and threw him to the ground, punching all the time. Eddie's father came and separated us. He sent Jeff in to pitch the rest of the game, and we lost 4–2.

CHAPTER
3

As soon as Mr. Gordon told us when he was holding our next practice, I took off. Just got on my bicycle and rode around. At first I thought I was getting lost, but then I passed Gino's and I realized that I wasn't very far from home.

Home. Hah, that was some joke. It was a nice enough house, I guess. The rooms were larger and the backyard sunny, but I still couldn't think of it as home. Home was the small ranch on Chestnut Street, about an hour's ride away. It was the only home I could remember; we'd moved there when I was just born. My friend Kenny lived around the corner and Billy was across the street. Boy, did I miss them. Mom kept promising she'd take me back there one Saturday so I could see them, but she never got the chance to, with all her errands and fixing up the new house.

I pedaled uphill, standing in order to get the bicycle to move. I was only a few blocks from the house, but I wasn't ready to go there yet. I was still steaming mad at Jeremy. I knew the real reason we had moved. Because of Jeremy. Everything always came back to Jeremy. Mom

18

had been saying the other house was too small and too dark, but one night I heard her talking it over with Dad. She thought that the school system here in Glen Haven was better and that Jeremy would get more out of their special classes. Well, big deal. Maybe he was getting more out of his special program, but I sure wasn't benefiting in any way.

The kids were all right, I guess. Pretty much like the kids where I used to live, except they had more toys and video games. But it was hard making friends. I tried to explain to Mom that by sixth grade kids were set with their friends. She said that was nonsense, that with my personality I'd have no trouble making new friends, because I was outgoing and interested in sports.

Well, she was wrong. The kids were nice enough in school. But that was it. Once the weather turned warmer I got into the habit of going over to the school yard and joining in ball games there. The kids always let me play, but it never went further than that. Of course I wondered if I were having trouble making friends because all the kids knew Jeremy was my brother. Eddie was the first guy to call me to get together.

I smacked the handlebar and hurt my fist. It was all Jeremy's fault. Why did *I* have to have a brother who was different? Even in my old school, as soon as people found out he was my brother, they'd snicker and smile that nasty know-it-all smile. Or worse, sometimes they'd make comments about "that retard." Jeremy wasn't retarded, but he sure could look and act weird. A long time ago, when I was five or six, Mom explained to me about his problems. "Neurological impairment" was the fancy term for why he acted the way he did. I guess deep down I knew that he couldn't help acting the way he did, and I felt sorry for him. But usually I forgot to, because he got me so angry most of the time—with all of the dumb things he pulled. Mom never should have put him on the same Little League team as me. In fact, he had no business being on *any* baseball team. He didn't even like baseball—or any sport, for that matter—and couldn't play if his life depended on it.

I rode into the school parking lot, a few blocks from our house, and watched some older boys playing stickball. Then, without even meaning to, I turned down our block and rode up the driveway. Both Mom's and Dad's cars were parked there. Suddenly it occurred to me that they could be worried about me. The game had ended almost an hour ago. And if I knew Mom, she'd be angry at me for going after Jeremy like that.

I put my bike in the garage and rang the doorbell. Nobody answered so I decided to go around to the back. There they all were, Mom stretched out on a lounge chair knitting, Dad and Jeremy planting vegetables. For a minute they didn't know I was there. I looked at the three of them, suddenly feeling they were strangers—a family I was watching, like in a movie—not people I belonged to.

". . . and you'll have to remember to water every few days," Dad was saying. "Especially if it doesn't rain much. Can you remember that?"

"Sure, Dad." Jeremy looked all excited.

"And we'll have to spray the plants soon to keep the insects away. Maybe I should do that."

"I can do it," Jeremy said stubbornly. "Just tell me which stuff to use and I'll take care of it. I *can*, you know."

"I know you can." Dad happened to turn and see me standing there. "Hi, Adam." He didn't sound angry.

"Hello, Dad."

Mom popped up from the lounge chair, her hand shielding her eyes from the sun. "So there you are," she said. "We were worried about you, disappearing like that."

"I just went for a ride," I mumbled.

Mom and Dad exchanged glances. They did that often when Jeremy was involved. I gathered they'd decided not to give me a hard time.

"I'm dropping out of baseball," Jeremy announced, as though nothing had happened between us. But that was Jeremy. He didn't hold a grudge.

"Good idea," I muttered under my breath.

"We'll talk about *that* later," Mom said firmly. "We only agreed that we'd discuss it, didn't we?"

"Yeah, but I told you. I want to drop baseball. I don't like it."

Dad sighed. "Helen, I think we should let Jeremy decide. Especially after what happened today."

Mom put her hands on her hips. "And we just finished saying that he'd give it another week or so. Jeremy has to learn not to give up every time something doesn't go right."

Something doesn't go right? With Jeremy things never went right.

"I'm not going to play another game," Jeremy insisted.

"We'll see," Mom said, having the last word.

.   .   .

It all didn't seem half as bad the next day, which was Sunday. For one thing, I could enjoy the rest of the Little

League season without Jeremy. My brother was the stubbornest person I knew, regardless of his problems. If he said he wouldn't play in another Little League game, I could take him at his word. I thought over what Eddie had told me—about his father making me starting pitcher—and decided that Mr. Gordon must have changed his mind. Coaches often did that the last minute. It wasn't *Eddie's* fault. I wouldn't even mention how disappointed I'd been. Eddie would probably tell me I was making a big deal out of nothing anyway.

Since we weren't going out for a while, I decided to call Danny and tell him I was free to come over and look at the drawings he'd made of the sets.

"Great!" he said. "Come right over. We can play some ball, too."

I jotted down his address and went into my room for my mitt. Dad was in the den reading the newspaper when I passed through.

"I'm going to Danny Martin's house," I told him. "He's a kid in my class and on my ball team."

"Fine," Dad said. "But be home by three. Your mother wants to go over to the mall and pick out carpeting for your bedroom."

I made a face but knew better than to argue. Mom believed that Jeremy and I should "take an active part," as she put it, in decorating our rooms. That way we'd have nothing to complain about later on. I guess she was right, but I hated shopping.

"All right," I agreed. "I'll be back by three."

Jeremy stopped me as I was getting my bicycle out of the garage. "Where are you going?" he asked.

"To visit Danny Martin."

"He's nice," Jeremy said. "Can I come, too?"

"No, Jeremy," I said firmly. "We're going to play ball and work on the sets."

"What sets?"

"For the sixth-grade play."

"I have nothing to do," he complained, frowning.

"Go work in your garden," I suggested. I didn't want him tagging behind.

"There's nothing to do, not even water." Suddenly his face brightened. "I know. I'll go for a ride on my bike."

I watched him push up the kickstand and wheel his bike out of the garage. I squeezed my hands together so I wouldn't grab his shirt and stop him. I knew that Mom and Dad didn't like him to ride around the neighborhood. They worried that he didn't watch out for cars. Sometimes I worried, too. But they were afraid to stop Jeremy because he would get very angry, saying, "Adam rides his bike all over, why can't I? I'm older, aren't I? And I'm not dumb, you know." And he was right, in a way. Even Mom knew she had to let him ride around sometimes.

"Can't you do something else?" I asked.

"No. What should I do?"

I shrugged my shoulders. I had no idea. "Well, tell Dad if you're going out." At least I wouldn't be responsible if anything happened to Jeremy.

"Okay," he said. "See you." Jeremy smiled and went back into the house. One thing about my brother: it didn't take much to make him happy.

. . .

Danny lived about five blocks away, on the other side of the school from my house. His mother opened the door as soon as I knocked. She seemed to be expecting me.

"Hi, Adam. Danny's in his room going over those

sketches of his for the hundredth time." She looked like Danny when she smiled. "I'm glad you're going to work on them with him."

"We'll have fun," I said, feeling comfortable with her right away.

"You're some pitcher," Mrs. Martin said. "I watched you yesterday afternoon."

"Thanks," I said, my ears growing warm from her compliment, and from remembering what *did* happen during the game.

Just then Danny's little sister came running past us, a bag of potato chips in her hand. "I'm taking these outside for Marnie and me," she told her mother. She was a cute kid, about eight years old, with red ribbons in her braids. She turned to me and started giggling. "Hi, I'm Michelle and you're Adam." Then, before I could say a word, she ran off.

Danny was sitting at his desk in the corner of his bedroom, staring at some papers in his hands. He looked up as soon as I came into the room.

"Hi, Adam. Take a look at these drawings and tell me what you think."

I looked at the three sketches. It was plain to see that one was a living room, one a garden, and the third an office. "Hey, they're pretty good!" I exclaimed, actually surprised at how good they were.

Pleased, Danny grinned. "I thought so, too, to tell the truth. Only"—he pointed at the office—"I can't decide if this should stay a door or if I should put in another file cabinet."

I studied the drawing. It looked fine the way it was. "I'd say leave the door."

"See," he said, "you're a big help already. And that takes care of that. Mrs. Casey wants to see them tomorrow so we can start working on the actual sets."

"She's nice," I said, picturing our thin, elderly art teacher who never raised her voice, even when the kids got rowdy.

"Actually, she's the one who suggested that I ask you to work with me," Danny said.

"She did?" I really wasn't that good at art.

"She said you had a good eye and that you could color between the lines."

We both had a good laugh over that one.

Danny got up. "Enough of this. Let's go outside and play ball."

We grabbed our mitts and a hardball and went to play catch in Danny's backyard. Then, after a while, Danny went into the house to get a bat and we took turns hitting. I liked playing ball with him. He didn't make any comments when I fumbled an easy pop-up. And I did belt out some good line drives, even though we were only tossing the ball up ourselves and hitting it. Danny told me he thought I'd make a good batter once I stopped stepping away from the ball during games. We started talking so much, I lost my concentration and hit the ball backward. It bounced off the wall next to the kitchen window. Mrs. Martin came right out, but she was nice about it.

"Why don't you two go across the street to the park where you'll have more space?"

"Sure, Mom. Sorry," Danny said.

"But come back in twenty minutes," she called after us. "I'm heating your pizza now."

"And if you're late, Marnie and I will eat it all up," Michelle added, giggling, suddenly sticking her head out the kitchen door.

"Fat chance, you little twerp," Danny yelled back. But I could see he wasn't even annoyed.

"I'm not a twerp, you ape man." The door slammed hard.

Danny laughed. "That kid. She's always mad because I'm older and she thinks everything I do and get is better."

I knew what she meant but I didn't say so. In my house I did everything better than my older brother. I even had to look out for him. But I still felt he got more attention because he was the firstborn as well as because of his problems.

The rest of the time passed quickly. Danny's father came home from his golf game with Mark's father and he complimented me on my pitching. After we ate our pizza and had ice cream pops, we played some Atari. It was a good thing that I happened to look up at the Martins' den clock. It was a quarter to three already! I said good-bye to everyone, thanked Mrs. Martin again for lunch, then rode home.

Later, in the car on the way to the mall, I told Jeremy how Danny and I spent the afternoon.

"He's a nice kid," Jeremy said. "Not like that Eddie Gordon."

"Eddie's all right," I said defensively.

"I'm glad I'm off his father's team. Eddie sure doesn't like *me*."

Mom turned around. "We'll see about that, Jeremy. Remember?"

"Look, I made up my mind," Jeremy said. "I'm not playing baseball anymore."

Dad cleared his throat. "I can't see the purpose of Jeremy staying on that baseball team, Helen. He doesn't enjoy it."

"That's not the point, Leonard." Mom spoke in her teacher voice. "He has to learn to stick to things. Not give everything up, like the guitar and karate and whatever else he's tried."

"Those were activities you picked out for him," Dad answered.

"Of course they were things I picked out," Mom said, getting annoyed. "He said he didn't care, that he'd try them. And then he didn't like them."

"I like gardening. And listening to the Beatles," Jeremy said.

Mom crossed her arms, then turned to look at Jeremy. "That's not what I mean," she said. "I'm talking about activities that involve other people. So that you get to know boys and girls your own age."

Dad sighed. "That's enough, Helen. Let's drop it for today."

I sighed, too. I hated that kind of discussion. Nothing was ever solved and it left everyone on edge.

I decided to change the subject. "Where did you go when you went out riding?" I asked Jeremy.

"No place special. First I rode over to the school and played on the swings."

Swings. I hadn't played on swings in years.

"And then I rode down Milton Road. There were a few kids outside so I stopped and played with them."

"How old were they?" Mom called out. She didn't like

it when Jeremy played with little kids, but they were the only kids that were willing to play with him.

"Oh, I don't know," Jeremy hedged, but we could all tell he was lying. "I—I guess they were in the third or fourth grade."

"Honey," Mom said, trying her sweet approach, "don't you think that's kind of young for a big boy like you?"

"They were nice," Jeremy insisted. "And they let me play with them. Especially Tommy. He invited me into his house when the others left, and his mother gave us peanut butter and jelly sandwiches."

"So that's why you weren't hungry," Mom said, "when I asked you what you wanted for lunch."

"And his mother told me to feel free to come and play with Tommy. Like a big brother." Jeremy laughed, pleased with himself. "I could tell that she liked me, too."

"I'm sure she did," Mom said slowly, "but I don't think it's such a good idea for you to go back there."

"Why not?" Jeremy demanded. "Mrs. Stein invited me back. And you and Dad keep telling me how I should only go to places where they invite me."

"Here we are," Dad said, turning into the enormous parking lot. "The mall looks kind of empty today."

"That's because everyone is someplace else having fun," I grumbled.

"That's enough, Adam," Mom said. "We can't always be off somewhere having fun."

Didn't I know it only too well?

CHAPTER

⊢——————⊣

4

Mom and Dad had a long talk that night, after Jeremy and I went to bed. I couldn't hear too much of the conversation since their bedroom door was shut, except that it had to do with Jeremy and baseball. The next morning at breakfast Mom told Jeremy that he was allowed to drop baseball so, as she put it, "he could devote more time to his studies."

Jeremy looked up from his bowl of cereal. "I study," he said.

"I know, dear. But in a month and a half you'll be taking finals for the first time ever. Don't you want to be well prepared?"

Jeremy just grunted.

"I'll call the guidance counselor during my coffee break," she told him, "and see if he can recommend a tutor to help you after school."

"I don't need a tutor," he mumbled. "Mrs. Fiore is my tutor in school, and so are Mrs. Anderson and Miss Brown." Jeremy went to junior high like the other seventh graders, but he spent most of each day in special classes.

Good to her word, Mom got a hold of "a wonderful woman" named Mrs. Dawson, who came and worked with Jeremy after school on Tuesdays and Thursdays. Jeremy grumbled and fussed that he didn't need another tutor, but Mom insisted that it could only help. When he appealed to Dad, Dad told him to try it for a few weeks and see how it went. That was Dad's standard answer to Mom's current Project Jeremy. But, to be fair, he did step in when he saw things weren't working out, like this baseball issue.

I guess deep down I felt sorry for my brother, constantly the subject of some harebrained scheme Mom would dream up. She wanted him to be like everyone else—play sports, get good grades. She couldn't seem to accept that Jeremy *was* different. I knew he was different but it still hurt at times. Like in the baseball games. I sure was glad that he wouldn't be embarrassing me there anymore.

I told Mr. Gordon about Jeremy's dropping out at our next practice. Eddie's father was short and wiry like Eddie, only his hair was a much darker red, almost brown, and when he took off his cap I could see it was thinning on top. But he still had good muscles; it was plain to see by the way he moved that he'd been a fine athlete when he was younger.

Mr. Gordon stared at me for a moment then said, "I understand, Adam. I suppose it's best all the way around."

I nodded. He reminded me of a sergeant in the army—strict but fair, although he did come down heavy on Eddie when he made an error, even in practice. I guess he just wanted his own son to be the very best.

Eddie realized that Jeremy wasn't at practice when

our half of the team was taking turns hitting. It was his turn at bat, then mine.

"Where's Jeremy?" he asked me.

"He dropped out," I said.

Eddie laughed. "Good move. Too bad he didn't do it sooner. Next he should think about dropping out of school and going to a place for dummies."

I walked away. I could hear Mark, who was playing catcher, say, "Hey, Gordon, you're a jerk. You know that?"

Then Eddie's voice, aggrieved. "What do you mean? Adam knows I'm only kidding." He came over to me and put his arm around my shoulders. "You know I'm kidding, don't you, Adam?"

I nodded, not knowing what else I could do. Eddie had become very important to me. I didn't want to risk losing his friendship by fighting over Jeremy.

Of course I didn't like it when Eddie made cracks about Jeremy, but I could understand why he and some other kids did it. Sometimes Jeremy just seemed to be asking for it—the funny way he walked, how he always looked sloppy. And those times he acted silly and had a giggling fit. I often wondered if Jeremy was looking for attention and didn't care that the only attention he got was being made fun of.

Besides, I knew that Eddie wasn't really mean or anything. And lately he'd been acting especially nice to me. He showed me how he threw his curveball and worked with me until I got it. And a few nights before I went over to his house for dinner. After we ate he went through his collection of baseball cards and gave me a big pack of doubles, almost thirty cards. When it came time for me to leave, I thanked Mr. and Mrs. Gordon. She was a real quiet lady. She hardly said a word during dinner. When I said good-bye to Eddie, he kept grinning and patting me on the back, like he was real glad to have me as his friend. Suddenly I wished that Eddie was my brother instead of Jeremy—Jeremy who never had helped me or taught me anything in his entire life.

Most school days around four o'clock, after Danny and I worked on the sets for the sixth-grade play, the four of us—Danny, Eddie, Mark, and I—would play softball in the school yard. Other kids started coming, too, and we'd have about six men on a side. Sometimes during the games I found myself hoping that nothing would go wrong for Eddie, because if things didn't go just so, he could blow his stack. Like the time Mark fielded his pop-up and caught it low to the ground. Eddie had reached first and insisted that the ball had touched the ground and that he was safe on base. But everyone told him he was wrong, even his own teammates. He didn't like it any better when Danny and I chimed in and said that Mark was right. He just narrowed his eyes and walked off the base. A shiver ran up my spine. Still, he was learning to keep quiet and not make a fuss about every little thing. I guess it bothered me to see him act like he had to make a hit every time he was up at bat. Where did he ever get such a weird idea? Even the professional ball players struck out and made errors. And Eddie was one of the best ball players around.

Jeremy couldn't stand Eddie. A few times he told me how nasty Eddie was to him in school—sticking out his tongue or making some comment about being dumb.

"Well, he's nice to me," I'd answer him. "If you don't like Eddie, keep away from him."

"Oh, I do," Jeremy said. "Far away."

Our team won the fourth game we played, giving us a record of two wins and two losses. The final score was 12–8. We were all proud because we knew that we'd hit and fielded well. I was especially glad because I hit a double in the second inning, not to mention that I struck out seven players—four in a row! I even helped make a double play. Boy, did the parents cheer. At the end of the game we whooped and jumped, patting each other on the back.

"Think you're so great, don't you, Krasner?" Eddie asked, smirking at me.

"Not bad," I answered modestly. "We're all pretty good, don't you think?"

"Yeah, we're all pretty good," he mimicked me.

"What's wrong now?" I asked him, but Eddie just walked away. What ticked him off like that? I shook my head, wondering. It took away some of the joy of victory.

Thank God Danny wasn't moody like that. He was cheerful and easy to be with. Mrs. Casey had given him the go-ahead for the sets and he spent part of every day after school drawing the outlines of the actual sets on enormous pieces of cardboard. At first Mrs. Casey kept looking over his shoulder, telling him to be careful. Danny kept assuring her that he *was* careful. After a few days she saw that he was doing a good job and she calmed down. She went about her own business, straightening up the art room, telling Danny to be sure to let her know if he needed her for anything. Finally she stopped staying there at all.

I don't know why I stayed there with Danny. He certainly didn't need me yet. I suppose I just liked being there with him. Sometimes we chatted while he drew—about school, about baseball. Once he told me that he

had wanted to be friendly with me when I first came into class, but that I seemed so aloof and unfriendly. I was so astonished, I didn't know what to say.

Other times, when I knew he was concentrating on something difficult, he didn't say a word. Just followed the pencil with one eye shut, his lips pursed into a circle. I had enough sense to keep quiet then, but I didn't mind. If it went on long enough I just took out my books and started my homework. But it never went on for too long.

Danny must have heard Eddie riling me after the game, because the following Monday, after making some comment about the other team not being that strong, he looked me straight in the eye.

"I sure hope you're not letting Eddie Gordon upset you by anything he says." He waited to see if I'd say anything, then he went on. "He can get pretty nasty when someone does something better than he does—like your pitching on Saturday."

I was too embarrassed to say anything. I cleared my throat. So what if I struck out one more person than Eddie did? Big deal. "Well, I don't know," I said.

"Well, I know and so does my cousin Mark. Eddie gets jealous over the least little thing. Mark used to be pretty friendly with him until he got sick and tired of Eddie's best-pal routine one day and insults the next."

Amazing. "I didn't know Mark felt that way," I blurted out. "I thought they were good friends."

"I know for a fact that Mark won't have anything to do with Eddie alone. Eddie knows it, too. But my cousin's not going to stop playing ball after school just 'cause Eddie's there."

"It must be hard on Mark, having Mr. Gordon as a coach."

Danny smiled. "Mr. Gordon's fair enough. Eddie must have asked his father to put Mark on the team months ago. And since we're all together, there's no point in making a fuss."

Danny went back to blocking out the sets. He was working on the last one, the office. It had lots of details and he was taking pains to do a good job. But I wasn't finished talking about Eddie.

"Do you hate Eddie, too?" I asked.

"I don't *hate* him," Danny said, still concentrating on what he was doing, "and neither does Mark. We just know enough to keep out of his way."

I thought a bit. "Boy, am I dumb. I thought you and Mark were good friends with Eddie. Like that time we all went to Gino's for pizza before the game."

Danny chuckled. "Eddie said the whole team would be coming and he especially mentioned you, so I said why not, since I wanted to talk to you about the sets anyway."

"That's funny," I said. "He couldn't have known that I'd be going when he told you that. But I'm glad we got together, even though we could have talked in school."

We both laughed at that one and I felt a little better. It still bothered me that Mark and Danny didn't really like Eddie, but it was a relief to know that he insulted other people—not just Jeremy and me. And I felt closer to Danny because he considered me his friend and didn't want to see me hurt. Not that I could understand why Eddie should be jealous of anyone.

I was very excited about our next baseball game because Dad didn't have to work that Saturday and was able to come and watch me play. We drove over to the field, just the two of us. Jeremy refused to go, so Mom gave in and took him for sneakers. The entire team got there early and we had a real good warm-up. As usual we all took turns hitting and fielding, then Eddie, Jeff, and I took turns pitching to Richie and Mark, our back-up catcher. Right before game time Mr. Gordon gave us a pep talk. He reminded us of how well we'd played the week before. Then he held up his clipboard and read out our starting positions.

"Adam, go to the mound. You're starting pitcher today. Eddie, play first base. Mark—"

"But, Dad," Eddie broke in, "I'm—"

"Go cover first base!" his father ordered.

"It isn't fair! I'm better—"

"Young man," Mr. Gordon bellowed, "if you want to play in this game, you better get your tail over to first base *right now*!"

Eddie shuffled over to first base and I stepped up to the pitcher's mound, a little less joyous than I'd been a minute ago. Sure, it was exciting to be starting pitcher for the day, but not at the cost of having Eddie mad at me.

Richie took his place behind the plate and I threw a few practice pitches. My arm felt good. The ball was going right where I wanted it to go. The first batter stepped up to the plate. I forgot about Eddie. I forgot that Dad was watching me pitch for the first time this season. I concentrated on every ball I threw.

My first pitch was a strike, which I took to be a good sign. The count went 1 and 2 and then the first batter struck out. An even better sign. The next kid up was Jimmy Layton, a sixth grader from my school who was good at all sports. He foul-tipped the first two pitches, let a high ball go by, then hit a line drive past Danny on third base. I turned in time to watch Jeff field it and throw the ball to Mark on second base. Mark ran toward Jimmy, who was trying to double back to first, and tagged him out. It was a great play and our team started clapping. Then I managed to strike out the next batter and all the parents on our side burst into applause. I couldn't stop grinning. I felt great and I didn't care who knew it.

The rest of our team must have been feeling pretty good, too. Eddie and Richie each singled and then Mark hit a triple, sending both of them home. We all roared and cheered. Anyone would have thought we'd won the game, the way we carried on. All of the commotion must have brought the other team to their senses because the coach put in a new pitcher and everything changed. Jeff struck out, Danny walked, one of the fifth graders hit a pop-up that the shortstop caught, and I struck out, ending the inning and leaving Mark on third base and Danny on first. We were ahead 2–0, but I felt kind of bad about striking out. I was still hesitating—afraid to connect with the ball.

But I had no problem with pitching. I tried out my new curveball and walked the first man up. Then I struck out the next two batters. The fourth man up was a mean-looking seventh grader who swung at everything I threw. On the count of 0 and 2, I threw him a fastball and he bounced it back to me. Holding my mitt low, I scooped up the ball and threw it to Eddie on first. He reached for it, but not far enough, and the ball sailed over his right shoulder, landing close to where my father was sitting. Eddie jerked around and ran after the ball, then threw it to second. Too late. The runner was safe. Mark threw it to me, a disgusted look on his face.

Eddie came running over to me, his face red with fury. "Thanks for the wild throw, Krasner." His voice was loud and sarcastic.

I was embarrassed, flustered, and sore. "But I didn't throw wild. You just didn't catch it."

"Yeah, we know. That's what *you* say. You're as dumb as your brother."

"Just keep my brother out of it. You're not so smart yourself if you have to blame your mistakes on other people."

At that, Eddie's face turned red. Before I could move he hauled off and punched me on the shoulder. Hard. I reeled from the pain. An arm reached out to steady me. It was Mr. Gordon.

"Are you all right?" he asked, concerned.

I nodded, afraid that if I spoke I'd say something stupid.

The umpire, a short, fat man, was glaring at Eddie. "Any further incidents like that and you're out of the game."

Mr. Gordon looked at Eddie. "I'll deal with you later. Now get back on base right now or I'll bench you myself."

Eddie headed for first base. Then he turned and gave me a strange smile. My hand formed a fist. Boy, did I want to get him back. Mr. Gordon cleared his throat. "I apologize for my son," he said. "Do you want to finish out the inning?"

"I sure do," I answered, sounding braver than I felt. I walked to the mound and Mr. Gordon returned to his coaching position near first base.

"Play ball," called the umpire.

I wound up to throw my first pitch, still shaky. I was positive that my throw to Eddie was good. And even if it wasn't . . .

"Ball two," the umpire called out.

I gritted my teeth and tried one of my fastballs.

"Ball three."

I looked around. Eddie was still smirking. Everyone else just stared back at me. Everyone but Danny. He gave me the all-right circle with his thumb and finger. What the heck, I thought, feeling a little better. I've nothing to lose. I concentrated and pitched a curveball.

"Strike one."

Another curveball. The batter decided to swing. He hit a fly ball near second and Mark was under it for the third out. Thank God the inning was over.

We won 4–2, our second win in a row. Boy, did our team cheer and yell—everyone, that is, except me. Mr. Gordon gave us a good pep talk, about how we worked together to win as a team. He spoke about "the unfortunate incident" that had better not happen again, all the time giving Eddie a dirty look. Eddie looked down at the ground while his father was talking, but the minute we were dismissed he grinned at me strangely, just as he had after his father had reprimanded him.

Dad offered to take me to Friendly's for an ice cream soda, and I said okay. We didn't talk in the car; Dad must have known I didn't feel like it. He always knew things like that.

We sat down in a booth and I ordered my usual—pistachio ice cream with hot fudge sauce and nuts. Dad ordered a cup of coffee.

"You're some pitcher," he said. "I'm really very proud of you."

"Thanks," I mumbled, suddenly shy. Dad wasn't one for compliments.

"I mean it." He smiled. "And just for the record, your throw to first base was good."

"Was it? I thought so, only—"

"Only that Eddie came on so strong, you began to wonder. He's some nasty kid, punching you like that. No wonder Jeremy doesn't like him."

"I can't understand why he'd do a thing like that," I said, shaking my head. "It's almost like he can't admit he's not Superman on the baseball field."

"Forget about it and eat your sundae. Your ice cream is beginning to melt."

I smiled, appreciating Dad's tact. But I couldn't forget about it. Eddie had changed. Everything had changed.

CHAPTER

5

I kept pretty close to home the next few days. Monday morning I dreaded going to school, but I couldn't turn into a complete hermit, could I? I expected everyone in school to look at me like I had two pairs of eyes. I mean, they must have heard about what happened between Eddie and me on Saturday. And although Danny and Mark didn't have a high opinion of Eddie, I could tell lots of kids thought he was pretty terrific. But no one said a word about it, not even Danny.

"I won't be able to work on the sets the next few days," he told me during lunchtime. "My sister and I have to stay at Mark's house this week because our parents went on a cruise."

"Oh," I said. I shrugged my shoulders as if I didn't care, but I really felt as though Danny were deserting me.

"I'll see you at the softball game," he said airily.

The softball game! I sure wasn't going to play in that game and let Eddie have another swipe at me. That strange grin he gave me twice let me know he didn't care what the umpire or his father had said. He'd get back at me. "I—I can't play this week. I have to help Jeremy with his work." Since we were in the same class, I couldn't very well tell Danny that I had too much homework.

Danny looked at me in a funny way, as if he knew I was lying. I could tell I was blushing from the way my face felt warm. Thank God the bell rang, marking the end of recess. Danny and I walked into the building, neither of us saying one word.

After school I walked home slowly, thinking that maybe I *was* making too much of what had happened Saturday. But I couldn't help it. Whenever some kid other than my friends Billy and Kenny from my old neighborhood started in on me, I just crumbled. Oh, sure, I said all the right things and even got into a few fistfights and held my own, but inside I always felt that the other kid came out ahead. That soon all the other kids would turn on me and make fun of me—like they made fun of Jeremy. I guess that's what came of having a brother like Jeremy. If someone hurt my feelings I withdrew. Like a turtle, my mother always said.

The house was unusually quiet since Jeremy didn't come home until three-thirty. I took some chocolate chip cookies and a glass of milk, then started on my homework.

"Oh, you're home," Jeremy said when he walked through the door.

I grinned. For some strange reason I was glad to see him. He looked sloppy as usual—his polo shirt half out of his pants.

"Boy, do I have a lot of homework," he said, dropping his books on the kitchen table. "Review, review, review. That's all those teachers know."

"I'll help you," I offered, glad to have something to do.

"How can you?" Jeremy asked, suddenly suspicious. "You're only in the sixth grade, remember?"

I goofed. Jeremy knew I could read and do math better than he could, but he hated to admit it. "Well, you show me what you have to do," I said, "and we could do it together. Like a game."

His face brightened. "Yeah, that would be nice. Too bad Mrs. Dawson doesn't come today. She's never here to help me when I really need her."

Jeremy put a cookie in his mouth just as the phone rang. He ignored the ring as he always did. But I didn't want to answer the phone. What if it was Eddie? It rang again.

"Answer it," I told him.

"You answer it," he mumbled through his half-chewed cookie. "I'm eating."

The phone rang again.

"Please," I said. "I won't help you with your homework if you don't."

"Oh, all right." Jeremy picked up the phone at the end of the fourth ring. "Hello," he said angrily into the receiver.

"I'm not home," I whispered, but he was too busy listening to the caller to hear me.

"Just a minute," he said into the receiver. Then he turned to me. "It's for you. Eddie Gordon."

"I told you, I'm not home," I said through clenched teeth.

"Just a minute," he repeated into the phone. At least he had the sense to put his hand over the receiver. "What do you mean," he asked me, "you're not home?"

"Just tell him I can't talk now."

I left the kitchen, not wanting to hear what he said to Eddie. After he hung up he followed me to my room.

"He said he'd call back later. Why didn't you want to talk to him? I thought he was your friend."

"I just didn't, that's all," I snapped. "Look, if you want me to help you, let's get started. And if Eddie calls again, tell him I'm not home or I'm busy or something. Understand?"

Jeremy shrugged. "It's your life," he said.

I reviewed some math with him, which was easy because it was really fourth- or fifth-grade level and this was the subject I was particularly good in. Then I got on my bicycle and went riding around the neighborhood. From a distance I could see the kids playing ball in the school yard. I wanted to stop and get into the game but I didn't. What if Eddie was there? He usually came down to play. I didn't want to see him or speak to him. I was sick and tired of his insults and angry that he hit me, but as far as I could see, there wasn't very much I could do about it except keep away. I didn't know how Danny and Mark managed to play ball with him and not get in the way of his temper. It was probably because Mark was bigger and stronger than he was, and Eddie knew he would stick up for Danny, too.

When I finally got home Jeremy told me that Eddie had called again, to see if I was going to play ball that afternoon.

"What did you tell him?" I asked.

"That I didn't know. That you were out riding your bike."

"Good."

"I still don't get what's going on here."

"That's all right," I told him. "Don't worry about it."

Thank goodness Eddie didn't call back that night. I mean, what could I say to him? Keep away—you hurt my feelings and I don't want to be your friend anymore? Naw. That was silly. I'd just avoid him as best I could.

. . .

The next afternoon Mrs. Dawson came to tutor Jeremy. She was a small, plump older woman who smiled a lot. From the sounds coming from the kitchen, I could tell she was making a game out of his reviewing—just like I did yesterday. Jeremy must have gotten fidgety toward the end of the hour because I heard her say, "You'll have to pay attention if you hope to learn anything." By the time she left, at four-thirty, she wasn't smiling anymore.

Jeremy let out a big sigh as he closed the door behind her. "Thank God that's over. But at least I got my home-work done."

"Me, too," I said. I suddenly realized that I didn't know what I was going to do with the rest of the afternoon.

Jeremy's face lit up. "Let's get out of here. Let's go visit Tommy."

"Who's Tommy?"

Jeremy was hurt. "Don't you remember? Tommy Stein. He's that little kid I met the first time you went over to Danny's house."

"I didn't know you still see him."

"Sure. Whenever I ride my bike I stop over there. He's usually reading outside his house. And now he waits for me, to see if I'll come."

I didn't say anything because I didn't want to hurt Jeremy's feelings, but who wanted to go and play with some little kid?

Jeremy tugged at my arm. "Come on and meet him. He's a nice kid."

I started to shake my arm loose and tell Jeremy to stop acting crazy, but I saw his face. He was all excited. He looked the way he did when he worked in his vegetable garden.

"All right. Let's go and see Tommy," I agreed. "I sure don't have anything better to do."

Tommy was sitting on his front steps reading comic books. He was skinny and small, small even for a kid in third grade, and his glasses kept sliding down his nose. As soon as he saw Jeremy he jumped up and ran toward him. I'd never seen anyone so happy to see my brother before.

"Hey, Jeremy," he shouted, hopping up and down, "I just knew you'd come today. We can finish our game of ghosts in the castle." Then he noticed me and began stammering. "Who—who's this? How come— I mean, I didn't know you brought someone with you."

"This is my brother, Adam," Jeremy said. He sounded proud of me. "He's a pitcher on his Little League team."

It was my turn to be embarrassed. "Yeah, well—hi, Tommy."

Jeremy laughed. I'd never seen him so delighted. "I finally got you two together. My two brothers."

Shyly, Tommy looked me up and down. "Does he like to play make-believe games, too?"

"He used to," Jeremy explained. "But now he likes sports."

"Not like us?" Tommy asked seriously.

"No, not like us."

We stood there, not knowing what to do next. Finally I

said, "Why don't you two go play your game? I'll stay here and read these comic books."

Jeremy looked at me questioningly. "You sure you don't mind?"

"Naw," I said, sorry I'd come with him in the first place. I couldn't help thinking about the softball game going on this very minute.

Jeremy looked relieved. "We usually play in Tommy's backyard. He has lots of trees and bushes to hide behind."

I sure didn't want to watch Jeremy making a fool out of himself, hiding behind bushes with this little kid. "I'll stay right here on the front steps," I said.

"Okay." Jeremy took off in his funny run, Tommy right behind him. Two strange ducks, I thought, and one of them has to be my brother.

I read the two Archie comics quickly. Again I had nothing to do. I decided to walk around to the back and tell Jeremy I was leaving.

My brother was standing over Tommy, his arms outstretched. He spoke in deep, ominous tones: "I will throw you into my dungeon and tear you apart, limb by limb, if you do not tell me where the jewels are hidden."

I almost burst out laughing. Thirteen years old and still acting like a clown.

Tommy was down on his knees. With his hands clasped together and his sad expression, he looked like he was about to cry. "Oh, please don't hurt me, Morgan," he whimpered. "I cannot tell you where the treasure is. It isn't mine and—" He broke off when he realized I was standing there watching.

"Sorry," I apologized. "I just came to tell you I'm going home."

"All right," Jeremy said in his normal voice. "See you later."

I rode home thinking about Jeremy and Tommy. Jeremy sure was weird, playing make-believe games with a little kid. But looking at it from his point of view, I couldn't blame him. He had no friends his own age. He didn't like sports or computers or board games. And there was little Tommy Stein, crazy about him. Even I could see that. Tommy actually looked up to my brother. He had to be the only person in the whole world who did.

Since I had nothing to do when I got home, I figured I'd tackle something Mom had been after me for weeks to take care of—cleaning out my junk. I started on my desk drawers, throwing out old pencils without erasers, last year's baseball cards, and other things. The waste-paper basket was half full, and I was about to start on my bookcase when I heard a noise behind me. I spun around. Mom was standing in the doorway.

"Hi," she said, smiling. "Whatever are you doing?"

"Cleaning out my room."

"Finally." She glanced at the junk I'd thrown out. Then, instead of being pleased like I thought she'd be, she frowned.

"Is everything all right, Adam? I mean, you don't usually stay home on a sunny afternoon to clean your room. Why aren't you outside playing ball?"

"I—I just didn't feel like it."

She looked at me closely. "Does it have anything to do with Eddie Gordon?" she asked. "Dad told me what happened during the game on Saturday."

"I guess. A little."

Mom made that funny sound through her nose that always meant she was exasperated. "I think you're being too sensitive. Kids always blame the next one when they've made a mistake."

I just nodded. Mom didn't know Eddie, how he could be nice one minute and nasty the next. "I'll probably play ball tomorrow," I said, just so she wouldn't go on about it.

"Where's Jeremy?" she asked.

"Out riding."

"Do you know where he went? I hate when he just rides aimlessly around. I worry that he won't watch out for cars."

"Don't worry," I said. "He's safe where he is." Too late. By trying to make Mom relax I got Jeremy into trouble.

"So he's over at little Tommy Stein's house again," she said, sighing. "And he knows how we feel about it, too."

"He's a nice kid, Mom," I said, trying to make up for squealing on Jeremy. "I met him today. He really likes Jeremy."

Mom looked me straight in the eyes. "Don't you think that your brother is too old to be playing with third graders?"

I blushed. My thoughts exactly. But I had to help Jeremy. "They like to play the same games."

Mom bowed her head and put her hand on her forehead. "You don't understand. With Jeremy's difficulties he needs someone who will teach him to behave appropriately. Not encourage him to act immaturely."

"Tommy's smart," I said.

"Thank God for that," she said and left the room.

• • •

That night we were just finishing dinner when Mom dropped her bombshell. She turned to my brother and said in her sweetest voice: "Jeremy dear, I really don't want to have to forbid you, but you must know that your father and I are not at all happy about your playing with that little boy. What's his name? Tommy?"

Jeremy turned on me, glowering. "Thanks a lot, pal."

"But I didn't—" I began.

"Don't blame Adam," Mom said calmly. "We discussed this very subject last week. Don't you remember? And you said that you would stop going there."

Jeremy's face turned red. "I know, but I like to go."

"Helen," Dad broke in. "Must we discuss this at the dinner table? I'd like to finish one meal in peace."

"You know very well that this is important," Mom snapped at Dad. "And it always falls into my lap, so I handle it when I can. It's as simple as that."

Jeremy turned to Dad. "Well, why can't I play with Tommy? He's nice and his mother likes me, too. She gives us a snack whenever I visit and tells me to come again."

Dad wiped his mouth and pushed his plate away. "You know that we'd be happier if you played with boys your own age."

"I'm sorry, Jeremy," Mom said, "but it's for your own good. You are not allowed to go over there anymore."

Jeremy banged his dishes into the sink and trudged up to his room. He slammed his door hard behind him. Dad sighed.

"I don't know, Helen," he said. "Sometimes I wonder if we're doing the right thing, always getting on his back."

Dad stood up and Mom smiled up at him. "Of course we are, Leonard. If we keep prodding him to be like the other kids, soon it should pay off."

Dad shook his head. "I think you're being overly optimistic. Dr. Rausch told us that we had to be realistic about what we could expect him to do."

"Oh, Rausch. That was at least two years ago. Things change."

Dad sighed but said nothing. We could hear the sounds of "A Hard Day's Night" coming from Jeremy's room. He'd turned the volume of his stereo all the way up like he always did when Mom got him mad. Dad went up to talk to him and I went down to the den to watch TV. Dad was being too kind when he said Mom was being overly optimistic about Jeremy. He was never going to be like other kids his own age. Not in a million years.

CHAPTER

6

*T*he next day in school, as our class was leaving the gym to return to our classroom, Danny was suddenly next to me. He wasn't smiling as usual and his eyes kept going from side to side.

"Do you still want to help me with the sets?" he whispered.

"Of course!" I said, forgetting to keep my voice down. "Why do you ask?"

"I guess because you've been acting funny the past few days. I thought you were mad at me or something."

"Are you kidding?" I stopped to stare at him and two boys walked right into me. Danny didn't crack a smile. He was serious. All this time I was upset about Eddie and Danny thought . . .

"No talking in the halls." Mrs. Hammel, our fussy old teacher, was glaring right at Danny and me. "Unless you both want to stay in for recess."

As soon as she turned around, Danny and I looked at each other and rolled our eyes.

"We have to work tomorrow and I mean really work," he whispered. "Mrs. Casey wants the sets done as soon as possible. Maybe I'll get Mark to help us."

"I thought you couldn't stay after because you're spending the week at Mark's house," I said.

"My aunt won't mind when I explain it to her."

"Fine," I said. "I'll be there."

For the first time that week I joined a softball game during recess. When the bell rang, Danny and I walked to our classroom together.

"Coming to play ball this afternoon?" he asked. "Try and make it, okay? Mark and I will be there."

"I guess so," I answered. I still didn't know if I would, but I was getting tired of hanging around the house with nothing to do.

"Good," Danny said, smiling. "We've missed you."

. . .

By the time I got home I figured I might as well play ball that afternoon. It was obvious that Danny still liked me. Mark, too, probably. I'd just keep out of Eddie's way. Then he'd have no reason to blame me for anything. I took some juice and cookies and started on my homework. No one ever got to the field before four o'clock.

Jeremy came home and went outside to water his vegetable garden. I watched him work, humming and smiling. I couldn't see what he was so happy about—only a few leaves had sprouted—but he was acting like his vegetables were sure to win first prize at the county fair. It was hard for me to understand how a few dumb plants could turn him on like that.

I was just sitting at the kitchen table, watching and wondering, when the doorbell rang. I got up and opened the door. Eddie was standing there.

"Hi," I said, too surprised to think of anything smart to say like "What are you doing here?" or "Get out of here."

"Aren't you going to let me in?"

"Sure." Automatically I stepped back so he could come into the house.

We both walked into the kitchen and stood there for a minute without saying anything. I sat down and looked at him. His mouth was working as if he were talking but the words couldn't come out.

Just then Jeremy came dashing up the steps from the den. "They're growing, Adam! All my plants are growing!" He stopped short when he saw Eddie. "Oh," he gulped, embarrassed.

"Hi, Jeremy," Eddie said.

Jeremy stared at him, then turned to me. "I'll be in my room if you want me." He left.

I felt like calling out to Jeremy and telling him to stay with me, but I knew that was ridiculous. Still, for some strange reason, I was glad he was around.

As soon as Eddie heard Jeremy close his bedroom door, he started talking, the words just pouring out of his mouth, one on top of the other.

"Look, I'm sorry I yelled at you that way on Saturday. It was real dumb, I know that. And I apologize for punching you like that. I shouldn't have gotten so angry."

"Yeah," I mumbled, not knowing what to answer.

"My dad's really mad at me. He said I couldn't play in this week's game if I didn't apologize to you."

So that was it! He was following his father's orders.

Eddie must have seen the look of disappointment on my face because his words came faster than ever.

"But it's not just because of him. I know I did a dumb thing and that I hurt your feelings. At this point I can't even remember who made the error, you or me, not that it matters. But I want you to know that I'm really sorry I acted that way." He put his hand in his pocket and pulled out a wad of cards. "Here. This is for you."

I looked at the cards he handed me. They were his baseball cards. I flipped through them. All the important players were there.

Reluctantly, I held them out to him. "I can't take these. It's your whole baseball collection."

He pushed my hand away. "I know what it is. I want you to have it."

"Yeah, well, I appreciate it, but I couldn't keep it."

"I *want* you to keep it. That's just the point. I was rotten toward you. You played great Saturday. I was jealous, so I made you feel lousy." His brown eyes studied me. "I bet you haven't been playing ball these past few days because of me."

"Well, I've been kind of busy," I said.

"Hey, Adam, I want us to be friends again, okay?" He grinned and tapped me on the shoulder. I couldn't help but smile back. But then I remembered how ugly he'd been that day, and then that weird grin. I put the pack of cards on the kitchen table.

"Look," I said, "I'm sorry, but I can't be friendly with someone who's nice one day and nasty the next. I just can't."

Eddie stared down at the linoleum. When he finally spoke he sounded like a little kid.

"I really can't blame you," he said softly. "Sometimes I get so angry I see red. I don't mean to get that way. But I'll try real hard to control it. Just tell me to shut up if I say anything mean again."

I sighed. What was the point of discussing it anymore? Eddie had come over to apologize and the cards were his peace offering. I could tell that he meant well even though he didn't always act well.

"All right," I finally said.

"Great! Let's shake on it." He held out his hand and we shook. That over, he grinned, all carefree again. "You coming to play ball this afternoon?"

"Sure," I answered. "Why not?"

"Well, then get your mitt and let's go."

Most of the kids were already there when we got to the field. We formed teams. "Hey," I shouted to Eddie as we took our positions at first and second base, "Danny and Mark aren't here. I wonder what's happened to them."

"They'll probably come any minute. Or maybe they're not playing today."

"He told me they were," I said, puzzled. Danny was usually one of the first kids at the field.

We played an entire inning and Danny and Mark never showed up. "That's strange," I told Eddie, as we walked back onto the field. "It's not like Danny to say they'll play and then not come."

"Forget about it," Eddie said. "They're probably busy with something else."

But it bothered me enough to call Danny after dinner at Mark's house. As soon as his aunt put him on I could tell that something was wrong.

"Something's happened," Danny said. He sounded angry. "Mark's in a lot of trouble."

"What's happened?"

"He's been grounded. For a week. My aunt won't even let him play in Saturday's game. And he almost got suspended from school for a few days."

"For God's sake, what happened?" I practically yelled into the phone.

"Mark was set up."

"Set up? You mean framed?" I almost laughed. Danny made it sound like Mark was in an old movie where the good guy gets framed for a crime he didn't commit.

"You heard me." Now Danny sounded like he was mad at *me*. "Mark would never spray Laura Lee Swanson's locker with shaving cream, would he?"

"Who's Laura Lee Swanson?"

"It doesn't matter. Her locker's next to Mark's. When she opened it at lunchtime to change books, everything inside was covered with shaving cream."

"So why did anyone think Mark did that?"

"Because while she was screaming and carrying on Mark came by and opened his locker. A can of shaving cream was sitting right there on the shelf. Laura Lee saw it and got more hysterical. She started screaming that Mark had ruined all her books and notebooks. And Mr. Helmsley happened to be walking by just then."

"God!" I exclaimed. Mr. Helmsley was the principal of the junior high. "What did he do?"

"Hauled Mark into the office and threatened to expel him. Mark started to cry. Then he called Uncle Murray down at the store and said he had to come and take Mark home."

"Boy. What did Mark say about all this?"

"Nothing, except that he didn't do it and that he had no idea how someone could have put the can of shaving cream in his locker. Laura Lee's locker was unlocked but his wasn't. And Mr. Helmsley's making him pay for a new social studies and math book."

"Sounds awful," I said, shuddering. Then I remembered how Mark always liked to clown around. "Are you sure that he wasn't just playing a little trick on her and it got out of hand?" I asked.

"I'm sure," Danny snapped. "Mark's my cousin and my friend. I know he wouldn't do any such thing."

I was sorry I'd made such a dumb remark. I couldn't imagine Mark's ruining someone else's books and I sure didn't need Danny mad at me. I tried to make amends.

"It sounds as though someone had it in for Laura Lee."

"Or had it in for Mark."

I thought about it. "Yeah, I see what you mean."

"Look, I gotta go now," Danny said. "See you in school tomorrow and we'll work on the sets afterward, okay?"

"Sure thing," I said. "And tell Mark that I'm sorry about what happened."

"Right. 'Bye."

I stared down at the receiver in my hand, dazed by what Danny had just told me. How could a kid be so rotten and do a thing like that and then frame somebody else? Poor Mark. To think how he must feel—being blamed for something he didn't do and getting punished for it, too. We were sure to lose Saturday's game if he couldn't play. It wasn't fair! Then I felt a twinge of envy. At least Mark had one good friend who believed in him—Danny. Danny believed his cousin in spite of everything and he expected everyone else to see it that way, too. I couldn't imagine anyone sticking up for me like that. Then I thought of something else. Would I have enough guts to stick up for someone like Danny was doing?

I had to talk to someone. I ran downstairs. Mom was in the kitchen stacking dishes in the dishwasher.

"I just spoke to Danny," I told her. "His cousin Mark got into trouble today for spraying some girl's locker with shaving cream. But Danny says Mark didn't do it. That he was framed."

"How do you know Mark didn't do it?" Mom asked calmly.

I was shocked. "Danny says he didn't. And he's a nice kid, Mom. You've met him."

"He did seem nice." Mom sighed. "These days it's so hard to tell who's nice and who isn't."

"Adam's right. Mark's a good kid."

I turned around and saw Jeremy standing in the doorway. I didn't know how much of our conversation he'd overheard.

"Did you hear what happened in school today?" I asked him.

"Some kids were talking about it in the halls."

Then I thought of something. "That's funny. Eddie didn't mention it either when he came over this afternoon."

"I'm not surprised," Jeremy said.

"What do you mean by that?" I asked, suddenly alarmed.

"Just that on the bus this morning he was busy doing his homework like always. Anyway, his knapsack fell. It was open and a can of shaving cream dropped out. I said something like 'I see you're shaving already, Gordon,' and he gave me this look. I mean, he really scared me. Then he said, 'Mind your own business, dummy,' and that was the end of it."

My heart was racing. "Yeah, yeah. That's some great

story," I taunted him. "You don't have to make up lies just because you hate Eddie."

"Adam," Mom said sharply. "Jeremy doesn't lie and you know it."

What I knew was that Jeremy wasn't good at lying, but I didn't say so. "Sorry, Mom," I said meekly. "But that doesn't mean Eddie did it and Jeremy knows it."

"That's why I didn't tell anyone about it," Jeremy said. "Except for now. Sometimes kids bring in shaving cream and spray it all over the mirrors in the boys' room."

"See what I mean?" I pointed out. "If you're accusing Eddie, then you're saying he deliberately got Mark into trouble. Danny says that Mark has to pay about fifteen dollars to replace the books that were damaged."

"Yeah, well, maybe Eddie didn't do it," Jeremy said, sounding unsure of himself. "I mean, I didn't see him go near Laura Lee's locker or anything."

"See, what did I tell you?" I shouted triumphantly. "You have no proof. No proof at all!"

Mom shook her head. "We have no way of proving who did it, one way or another. All I know is that it's a rotten shame that *anyone* would do something like that."

"Probably some crazy did it," I said. "Someone we don't know."

Jeremy and Mom looked at me. They both seemed on the verge of saying something, but neither of them said a word.

CHAPTER
7

I didn't hear much more about the incident with Mark and Laura Lee and the shaving cream. Only that he was grounded for a week and ended up paying just five dollars in fines, since the books weren't really damaged after all. Still, it was a stiff penalty to pay for something he didn't do. Of course our team lost the game Mark wasn't allowed to come to, just as I expected. Danny said that Mark was especially mad about that.

The school play was in two weeks and Danny and I worked on the sets every day after school. These two girls—Patty Shore and Michelle Briar, who were in the play but didn't have big parts—started to come by the art room, so we let them help us paint until it was time for them to go on stage. Then they'd rush away to the auditorium, saying that they'd be late and that their teacher, Mr. Landon, who was in charge of the play, would kill them if they missed their cues. Michelle had blue eyes that kept staring at Danny and curly blonde hair that bounced when she walked. But I really thought that Patty was nicer, even though she wasn't as pretty. When she smiled at me I got the feeling that she could see inside my thoughts and liked what she saw.

A couple of times the girls came back after they'd rehearsed their parts. Then the four of us sat around and talked. Danny and I forgot about the softball game, but neither of us cared. Besides, now that we were winning more baseball games, Mr. Gordon held weekly practices at our school field. We'd just moved into fourth place. If we kept our position, we'd make the play-offs.

"Where have you been all this week?" Eddie asked me during our next practice as we jogged around in a large circle. "Turning into a hermit?"

"I've been busy working on the sets for the play," I told him. I felt nervous, like he was going to get mad and think I'd been avoiding him, but he just smiled. Ever since we'd made up he'd been on his best behavior with me.

"Why don't you take a break tomorrow?" he called over his shoulder as he sprinted ahead. "If you want, I'll come over and we can practice your knuckleball."

"Great!" I shouted.

"I'll be over as soon as I get home from school," he promised.

The next day Jeremy was just finishing his snack when Eddie came by.

"We're going over to the school yard to work on my knuckleball," I told Jeremy.

"Good," he said, looking Eddie straight in the eye. "I'll be busy around here and I don't want you hanging around."

Eddie flinched and looked away. I tried to think of something to say. Sure, Jeremy had every reason to hate Eddie for all the mean things he always said to him. Still,

I felt embarrassed for Eddie. For some dumb reason I noticed how much bigger Jeremy was than Eddie. Jeremy was a good size for his age and pretty strong, even though he wasn't athletic. But I don't know why I was thinking like this. Jeremy almost never got into fights—unless someone pushed him too far.

I decided to make a joke out of it. "What are you doing that you need so much privacy? Making a bomb?"

"Ha ha," Jeremy answered, not at all amused. "First, I'm going to water my plants and then I think I'll go bike riding."

Now it was his turn to be embarrassed. I knew he was going over to Tommy's house. He never actually told me and I didn't need to ask. I could just tell, by the way he'd slink off, then come home hours later, laughing and singing his fool head off.

"Have fun," I called out as I grabbed my mitt from the hall closet.

Eddie didn't say anything until the door closed behind us. "Wow, does your brother have some chip on his shoulder."

I couldn't let that go by. "Well, maybe he's sick and tired of people making fun of him and calling him names."

Eddie laughed. "Yeah, well, maybe he can't take a joke."

I didn't answer. As far as I could see, Eddie was wrong. But anything I'd say about it wouldn't change his way of thinking. We were friends again now, and he helped me in ways Jeremy never could in a million years.

The school field was empty except for a group of small kids playing soccer at the far end. We started working on my knuckleball. I was having trouble gripping the ball with my knuckles. Eddie kept showing me how to do it. I wondered how he managed it so well, since his hands weren't much bigger than mine. He could throw every pitch—sidearm, curve, change-up, knuckle. Only he couldn't throw as many strikes as I could. I guess that was why his father had been making me starting pitcher in the last few games. That and the fact that Eddie was a terrific first baseman.

I couldn't get the knack of holding the ball correctly, then throwing it strong. Eddie was becoming impatient. His face was turning red. Finally he told me to hold the ball by the tips of my fingers. "Try it this way," he said, and I did.

"Not bad," he admitted when I'd thrown a few. "Maybe your hand is too small to throw from your knuckles. Keep doing it this way for now."

"Okay," I agreed, surprised that it was finally working.

"Dad had me throwing like this last year," he said. "I guess I should have started you off this way."

I threw him a few more knuckleballs. I was just getting the hang of it when I noticed some kids walking toward us. It was Bobby Reese and Jason Marconi, two of the boys who usually played in our softball game.

Eddie must have seen them, too, because a minute later he said disgustedly, "Here they all come. Now we'll never have a minute to ourselves."

"Don't you want to play today?" I asked hesitantly. Somehow, I'd just assumed we'd play in the game when all the kids arrived.

"I thought you wanted to work on your knuckleball. I thought that's what we planned to do today." He sounded hurt, like I was disappointing him.

"Sure I do," I said quickly. "Let's go. We can work on it in my backyard."

"Great idea," Eddie said, suddenly cheerful again. "If you're going to be our team's starting pitcher, you have to have every pitch down cold."

I smiled, glad that he wasn't jealous of me anymore on that account. Being jealous of me was just plain dumb. Eddie was a better all-around player than I was. How could he not know that?

Jeremy was wheeling his bicycle out of the garage when we got back to the house.

"The kids started coming for the softball game," I told him, "so we decided to come back here and work on my pitching in the backyard."

"Watch out for my garden," he said, and he was off.

Our backyard was pretty much like all the others in the neighborhood—a terrace outside the den for sunning and barbecuing, then a lawn with a few trees bordered by bushes. Only most of our lawn was taken up with Jeremy's garden—at least the whole right side of it was.

"Look at that garden," Eddie said, whistling through his teeth.

It was pretty impressive. Jeremy had planted lettuce, tomatoes, green peppers, and corn, all in large amounts.

"It's Jeremy's," I said. "He's real proud of it."

"Oh."

Eddie walked away from it as though it was suddenly a mess of poison ivy. "Sure takes up a lot of room, doesn't it?" He laughed nastily.

I positioned myself next to the garden and waved my hand for Eddie to move farther down.

"Now be careful," he said in falsetto. "Be sure not to step in your brother's precious garden."

I was sick and tired of his gibes, especially since I was suddenly afraid that he might try and ruin Jeremy's garden out of spite. "That's enough, Eddie," I snapped. "Let's just leave my brother out of this."

As soon as the words left my mouth I regretted saying them. Now Eddie would blow his stack and go home. But to my surprise he only shrugged his shoulders and said, "Let's play ball."

The first knuckleball that I threw was a strike. I was glad. And I was glad that I'd finally spoken up to Eddie and nothing happened.

After a while I got tired of pitching and we had a great time just horsing around. We made up a hit-and-tag game for two people—something like spud—and that's when it happened. I hadn't realized that we'd gotten so close to Jeremy's garden until I heard a crunch and felt something like twigs under my feet. When I looked down I saw two of the young pepper plants were under my sneakers. I'd also knocked over a few stakes that propped up the tomato plants, which were just starting to grow.

"Oh, God, look what I did." I jumped out of the garden as if my feet were on fire.

"Hey, with that kind of height you can become a high jumper," Eddie said.

"It's not funny," I said. "Jeremy's going to be real upset." I knelt down to look at the plants. The stems of two tomato plants were broken and the peppers were badly damaged. They all refused to stand upright. I tried to pack dirt around them like I'd seen Jeremy do, but it didn't do any good. They just flopped down toward the ground. I felt awful. Jeremy loved his garden and now I'd gone ahead and ruined four plants.

"I don't know what to do," I said finally, standing up. "Jeremy's going to be real upset about this."

Eddie patted my shoulder. "Don't worry about it. I mean, it's not as if we did it purposely. You tried to be careful, didn't you? Accidents always happen."

Was he making fun of me? For a minute I wasn't sure.

"I just wasn't careful enough," I said. "I mean, I was watching to make sure I didn't step in his garden, but then we were having so much fun . . ." I finished lamely, knowing it was no excuse. I *should* have been more careful and I hadn't been. Boy, was Jeremy going to be mad at me when he saw what had happened.

"I think you should give them a good watering," Eddie said. "I mean, everyone knows water is good for plants and helps make them grow. I bet it will revive these sad sacks."

I looked at him questioningly. "Do you really think I should?"

Eddie nodded firmly. "I really do."

I got the watering can from the garage. Eddie took it from me. "Here, let me do it."

Before I could say a word, he was dousing the injured plants but good. "That should do it," he said.

I knelt down to see the results. If anything the plants looked worse—drooping and falling into the mud.

Eddie poked me and I almost fell into the whole mess. "Look," he said, "I think you better leave them alone. Those poor plants look like they're drowning." He started to laugh.

"Yeah, you're right." I just stood there, not knowing what I could do. I mean, there was nothing else to do—now.

"It's best to just forget about those plants," Eddie advised. "They're goners."

When I didn't answer, he said, "Hey, let's go over to the school and get into the game."

"Naw, you go," I said. I really felt bad.

"I'll stay here with you, if you like."

I looked at him, surprised. "Okay. We may as well play some Atari."

We sat down in the den and started playing Donkey Kong and then Pac-Man. At first I couldn't concentrate and Eddie kept winning. But soon I forgot about the plants and we were neck and neck. I was so engrossed in the game that I didn't hear the front door.

"Who's there?" I called up when I heard footsteps in the kitchen.

"It's me," Jeremy answered.

"Oh," I said and went back to the game. I heard Jeremy go upstairs to his room. A little while later I heard the kitchen door slam. Just then I remembered the plants. I looked out the glass door and saw Jeremy running toward me, his eyes popping, his lips twisted with rage.

"What happened to my plants?" he screamed as he ran into the den. "They were fine when I left. Now they're all stepped on and drowning."

I opened my mouth to speak but before I could say one word, Jeremy was standing over Eddie, his hands making fists.

"You ruined them, didn't you? I know you did!" he screamed.

"Take it easy," Eddie said, getting up from the couch where we were sitting. "It was an accident."

Jeremy pushed him back down. "Yeah, some accident. I know about you and your accidents." His face was all scrunched up. I thought he was about to cry.

"It *was* an accident," I said. "We were playing ball and I stepped on your plants. I'll pay you back so you can buy some new ones."

Jeremy turned on me. "It's too late to buy new plants. And stop lying to protect this little creep. I know he did it just as I know he put the shaving cream in Laura Lee's locker."

At that Eddie jumped to his feet, ready to kill. "You take that back, Krasner," he snarled at my brother.

"I will not," Jeremy said. "I saw you with the shaving cream that day and I'm going to tell Mr. Helmsley so tomorrow."

Eddie laughed at him. "Yeah, you and who else? He won't believe a re-tard."

"Stop calling me a retard."

I saw Jeremy's hands go around Eddie's neck and I got scared. I pounded Jeremy on the back until he let go.

"Cut it out, both of you," I yelled. "I stepped on your precious plants, Jeremy, and I already told you I was sorry."

Jeremy fixed his eyes on me. He seemed to be figuring something out, then he said, "And you'll be sorry, too." He stomped out of the room.

Eddie left right after that and Jeremy and I each stayed in our own room until Mom came home. Then each of us, separately of course, went to tell her his side of the story. I told her how sorry I was, but that Jeremy had no right to turn on us that way.

Mom sighed deeply and brushed back a strand of hair from her forehead. I could see that she was tired from standing all day at the bank.

"I'm sorry it happened, too," she said. "You should have told your brother about it as soon as he came home."

"I know," I agreed. "Only I forgot for the minute. Eddie and I were playing Pac-Man."

"Your brother's garden is more important than a game," she said sternly. "It's the only thing he cares about in this world. You know that."

"You're right," I answered meekly. "I did offer to pay for new plants."

"Jeremy says it's too late for planting," Mom said. "I think what really got him mad was that you tried to drown them."

"We thought water was good for them. What do I know about plants?"

Mom patted my arm. "All right, Adam. Go wash your hands and set the table. I'll talk to Jeremy after dinner."

Dinner was a silent affair for the three of us, since Dad was working late. For once Mom made no attempt to draw us into conversation. Jeremy ate his food even more noisily than usual. Sometimes I'd catch him staring at me, scowling. When he did that I'd just look down.

I helped Mom clear the table and then went down to the den to watch TV. There wasn't any ball game on that evening so I flipped through the channels. Nothing. How did they expect a kid to get through the evening?

I decided to go to my room and put my baseball collection in order. As I walked up the stairs I heard Jeremy running and then his door slam. I took one look in my room and screamed.

"Mom, Mom, come here!"

"What is it, Adam?" She sounded frightened as she hurried up the stairs.

"Just look," I said, making no attempt to stop the tears rolling down my face. "Just look what he did. That moron!"

We both stared down at my floor. Jeremy had taken all of my baseball cards and ripped them in half.

8

*M*om and Dad punished Jeremy for what he did. First of all, he had to apologize to me, which was something I could have done without. I mean, who cared if he said he was sorry? He'd deliberately ripped up my cards, hadn't he? Also, he was grounded for a week. I made it my business to keep out of his way, but whenever he passed me on the stairs or in the hall, he gave me a dirty look and started mumbling under his breath. When I complained to Mom about him, she let out a deep sigh and said something about his difficulties being a constant burden to him and his level of frustration reaching its breaking point when I'd stepped on his plants. I just nodded as if I understood, which I did in a way, but all the old disappointments and grievances I'd always felt about Jeremy just came into my mind. The baseball cards were the last straw. The next day I noticed that he'd put chicken wire around his precious garden. Too bad he hadn't done it sooner. It would have saved us all a lot of trouble.

I decided to pretend that I didn't have a brother. That I was an only child and that Jeremy was some kid my parents had taken in because he had no home and they'd felt sorry for him. I suppose it was a terrible thing to make up, but what good was Jeremy? I couldn't play sports or games with him or even talk to him. And as an older brother he was the pits. He never could help me with anything; in fact, I knew about more things than he did. *I* had to help him, and that wasn't the way things were supposed to be. All he did was embarrass me. No wonder the other kids laughed at him. I'd just keep out of his way. And since it was the middle of June, that was an easy thing to do.

I called Eddie a few times, just to talk. I laughed when he made jokes about Jeremy—even when he said my parents should send him away to a school that had locks on the doors and bars on the windows. It felt good while he was still on the phone, but I felt rotten about it as soon as he hung up. Once or twice I wondered if Eddie had deliberately drowned Jeremy's plants. But I knew it was a dumb thought and put it out of my mind.

The school year was winding down. As sixth graders, we hardly did any work anymore. It seemed we had an activity every other day, which was nice, since I was finally being included. First we had a picnic with the sixth-grade classes of the other two elementary schools in our district. We all had to bring our own lunch. Somehow or other, Danny and I got to sharing a blanket with Patty and Michelle. It turned out to be a good idea because we pooled all of our food and the girls had lots of cookies and cake. Just as we were through eating, two boys we'd played against in Little League came over to compliment me on my pitching. I could feel my ears growing warm and knew I was blushing because the girls were listening. When the boys left Danny grinned.

"Well, what do you know," he said. "We have our own Ron Guidry right here on our blanket."

I punched him in the arm and we ended up wrestling, the girls laughing the whole time. It suddenly hit me that I no longer felt like the new kid in school. People knew me; I had friends! I got so excited, I threw myself on Danny with all my might and managed to pin him to the ground.

The picnic only lasted an hour. The buses came to take us back to our school. Patty sat with me and Danny and Michelle shared the seat behind us. Patty and I didn't talk much, but I liked having her next to me. I couldn't wait until the sixth-grade party, which was right after graduation. It was being held in our school cafeteria with a live disc jockey running the show. I made a mental note to remember to ask Danny if he knew how to dance, so he could teach me just in case I felt like asking Patty.

We were almost finished with the last set. Mrs. Casey wanted them all done a week before they put on the play so that everything would be ready without any rushing at the last minute. As we were putting the finishing touches on all the details, Mark ran into the art room, panting with excitement.

"Did you hear what happened with your brother and Eddie?" he asked me.

A tingle of fear ran up my spine. "No, how could I? I haven't been home yet. What happened?"

"They had a fight in the junior high cafeteria."

"Jeremy?" I couldn't remember the last fight he'd gotten into, if you didn't count the squabbles he had with me and Mom.

"Yep, Jeremy." Mark was grinning, like my brother had

just won a prize or something. "And he gave it but good to that creep. Eddie was crying when the gym teacher came over and broke it up."

"Why were they fighting?" Danny asked.

"Eddie pulled his usual. Insulted Jeremy as he walked by with his lunch tray. Called him a retard. Jeremy put down his books and his tray and punched Eddie in the mouth."

I was afraid to ask but I had to know. "What did they do to Jeremy?"

"Called your mother, I think, and Mrs. Gordon. And I heard both of them had to stay in for detention."

I had two feelings inside me which kept getting mixed up as each tried to cancel the other out. First of all, mad as I was at him, I was glad that Jeremy finally got back at Eddie, and proud that he'd knocked him down. But I was afraid. Terribly afraid. Knowing Eddie like I did, I was sure that this wasn't the end of the incident. I just knew that he was going to retaliate and do something horrible. Jeremy was my brother, but Eddie was my friend, and for some stupid reason, I felt like I was in the middle of it all.

I got up from the floor where Danny and I had been working. "I better go home. I should be there when Jeremy comes in, I guess."

Danny nodded, understanding. "See you tomorrow. We can finish this then."

Jeremy walked into the house about half an hour after I got home. I was in the den when he unlocked the front door. I heard him go into the kitchen and throw his books on the table. I ran up the stairs.

"Hi," I said, suddenly nervous.

"Hi," Jeremy answered. He took a container of Tropicana out of the refrigerator and started drinking from it.

"Don't do that," I said before I could stop myself. "Mom will be mad."

"Mom's not here and I'm just finishing it up." He tossed the container toward the sink, about a foot from where he was standing. It fell on the floor. Disgusted, he picked it up and put it into the garbage.

"I had a fight with Eddie Gordon today. Mr. Helmsley made us stay after for detention." He spoke as if it was no big deal, like it was something that happened every other day.

"I know."

He gaped at me. "Who told you? Mom?"

"Mark. He stopped over at school while I was working on the sets."

"I guess everyone knows about it." He didn't sound proud or embarrassed, just matter-of-fact.

"What happened?" I asked. "Mark said he called you a name."

"Yeah, and I just about had enough of him so I let him have it."

"Is Eddie okay?"

"Yeah!" Jeremy was suddenly angry. "What do you care so much about him for? I'm your brother. Don't you care that he insults me all the time?"

"Sure I do," I answered, feeling guilty. I'd never told Eddie to stop insulting Jeremy, since I knew it wouldn't make any difference, except to get him mad at me. But I couldn't help it. I liked Eddie, in spite of his faults.

"He's a jerk," Jeremy said sullenly. "It's about time somebody put him in his place. I don't know why someone didn't do it sooner."

"Yeah, well," I began, "but to hit him like that."

"He's no good," Jeremy went on. "I *know* he put that

shaving cream all over Laura Lee's locker and I told him so again. He did it because he doesn't like her and to get Mark in trouble."

"What does he have against Mark?"

"I heard some kids say that he tried to be good friends with Mark—taking him to ball games and stuff like that. Until Mark got sick and tired of his turning nasty for no reason at all and told him to get lost. So Eddie got even by making it look like Mark sprayed Laura Lee's locker."

"I can't believe that," I said.

Jeremy looked me straight in the eye. "You know, in some ways you're a lot dumber than me."

"Thanks," I said angrily.

"If you're so smart," he said, "you'd never have gotten mixed up with Eddie Gordon."

"That's how much you know," I said loudly, to make my point. "Maybe there's a side of Eddie that you don't know about. For example, how he was the only kid around here to become my friend. I didn't notice anyone else taking the trouble to include me in until he did."

"Did you ever stop to think, Mr. Smarty Pants, that maybe Eddie got friendly with you because he has no friends? He sits alone in the cafeteria and on the school bus." And with that, he stomped out of the kitchen and up to his room. He slammed the door so hard I was sure it would come off its hinges.

Mom came home soon after that and went upstairs to talk to Jeremy. Dad had a talk with him, too, after supper. Finally, around nine o'clock, Jeremy came down to watch TV in the den with the rest of us. As far as I could see, he didn't seem at all upset.

"Did they ground you again?" I asked when Mom and Dad went into the kitchen for a second cup of coffee.

"Nope," he said, grinning. "They don't care what Mr. Helmsley says; they don't blame me one bit for what I did."

I couldn't help grinning. "I must admit you probably gave Eddie the shock of his life when you smacked him one."

"Right on the kisser," Jeremy said, swinging his fist. "Right on the kisser."

I watched some TV, then took a shower and got ready for bed. Mom called up around a quarter after ten for me to put the light out, that I had school the next day, like she always did. I lay there in the dark, not at all tired. I couldn't stop thinking about the fight between Jeremy and Eddie. Somehow, even though I hadn't been thinking about it much all evening, I knew it was of special significance to me. It had a greater effect on me than even the time that Eddie had claimed I'd thrown him a wild ball and punched me.

Maybe up until now I'd refused to look at the rotten things Eddie had been doing all along because I was flattered that he wanted me as his friend. I felt a twinge of shame. All along Eddie had been insulting Jeremy— calling him names and provoking him—and I hardly ever even tried to stop him.

But Eddie was especially nice to me, I reminded myself. He worked with me on my pitching and gave me baseball cards.

I glanced at my clock. It was a few minutes past eleven. Suddenly I wanted a glass of milk. I got out of bed and walked past my parents' room. The door was closed and I could hear the sound of the TV. Downstairs, I was surprised to find Dad drinking a cup of coffee at the kitchen table.

"Still up?" he asked.

"I couldn't sleep."

"Do you want to talk about it?"

"I guess so," I said, not sure where to begin.

Dad said nothing. He was good that way, knowing when to stay quiet.

"I wish I didn't have a brother like Jeremy. I wish I had someone normal. Someone who could play ball and . . ." Crying, I crept into my father's lap.

Dad held me until I calmed down. I never expected to say those things! They just came out.

"Sorry, Dad. I didn't mean . . . I mean, I love Jeremy. He's my brother, but . . ."

Dad patted my back. "Don't apologize for your feelings, Adam. Your mother and I wish that Jeremy could function like other thirteen-year-olds, but we know he can't. It's hard on all of us, but hardest on Jeremy. He knows, better than any of us, how hard it is to live in a world where everyone can do things he has to struggle with."

"I guess so." I thought of Jeremy having so much trouble with his school work and knowing that he had no friends because he was different. I wondered how it must feel to *know* that you couldn't do lots of things kids even younger than you could handle easily.

"Then there's Eddie," I said after a while. "I don't know what to do about him. He's my friend, and then I think—how could I have him as a friend when he's so nasty to my brother." I looked Dad in the eye. "Do you think I should stop being his friend because of how he treats Jeremy?"

Dad sighed. "I suppose it would be easiest for you if I told you not to be his friend, but that's not how it works.

It's up to you, Adam. You have to choose your own friends and be able to decide if a person isn't for you. My telling you not to see Eddie is like telling you how to feel about him."

I thought about it. It was up to *me* to decide whether or not I wanted to keep Eddie as a friend.

Dad laughed. "Don't look so serious, Adam. I have faith in you that you'll come up with an answer."

"I guess one thing I *do* know is that, no matter how he is, Jeremy is my brother, and I'll stick up for him."

Having reached this conclusion, I yawned.

Dad stood up and patted my shoulder. "I think you'll be able to sleep now."

"Thanks, Dad." I hugged him and went up to my room. It was only as I was drifting off to sleep that I realized that I never had my glass of milk.

. . .

But Jeremy's victory didn't last very long. The next day he left for school before I did. I was eating my cereal when he ran back into the house, swinging something long and furry from his outstretched hand.

"Look at this!" he shouted indignantly. "Just look at this!"

"Ick! Get that away from me!" I shouted. Mom gasped. It was a small squirrel. Dead. A string was tied tightly around its neck, from which hung a sign saying "For the re-tard."

"That no-good, rotten Eddie Gordon," Jeremy sputtered, barely able to get the words out. "Can you believe he did this?" he asked incredulously. "He's mad at me so he goes ahead and kills a poor, innocent squirrel."

I was disgusted. So were Mom and Dad.

"I'll have a word with his father," Dad said.

"But Leonard," Mom protested, "we have no proof."

We all turned to her, frowning.

"Well, it's true," she said shakily but firmly. She looked at me. "And he's your friend, Adam, isn't he? Would Eddie really do a thing like this?"

"No. Maybe. I—I don't know," I said, suddenly confused.

Dad went and got a shoe box and put the dead squirrel inside. "Go catch your bus, Jeremy. I'll dispose of this and your mother and I will decide what we're going to do." He looked at me. "And you finish your breakfast, if you can."

I was steaming mad about the dead squirrel all the way to school. What a horrible, disgusting thing to do. Jeremy had to be right about Eddie and Laura Lee's locker. But the squirrel. Ick! That was even worse. This was it, as far as I was concerned. Eddie was no longer my friend. I thought about him and all the good things he'd done for me, like helping me with my knuckleball and giving me baseball cards and being my friend when no one else was. I felt like crying. No matter how many bad things he'd done, it still hurt to lose a friend.

I didn't get a chance to tell Danny about the squirrel until our class went to the library.

"What are you going to do about it?" he whispered.

"I'm going to talk to Eddie this afternoon. At practice."

"What good will that do?" Danny asked. "He'll only deny it."

Suddenly Mrs. Hammel was standing between us. "Daniel and Adam, do you wish to stay in with me during recess?"

"No, Mrs. Hammel," we answered contritely.

"Then conduct yourselves properly in the halls," she said severely.

I looked down but not before I caught Danny's wink.

That afternoon we put the finishing touches on the office set. Mrs. Casey stopped by and said it was a terrific job. Then we grabbed some kids to help and carried all three sets to the auditorium, where they were rehearsing the play. The cast stopped saying their lines while we leaned the sets against the back of the stage. Mr. Landon, Patty and Michelle's teacher, stood with his hand on his hip watching us. As we were leaving he let out a dramatic sigh and told the kids to go on with the rehearsal, since there couldn't possibly be any further interruptions. In the hall Danny and I looked at each other and burst out laughing. We were a full five days ahead of schedule. We grabbed our books and left the school.

But we were back an hour later for our last baseball practice. Saturday was the last game of the season and if we won it we'd be in the play-offs. Then there was still the All-Star game next Thursday night. Mr. Gordon had to select four players from our team to play in the game. I had a pretty good chance of being one of the four players, but, as I saw it, it was a toss-up between Jeff and me and Jeff would get it, being a better hitter and fielder than me.

I felt butterflies in my stomach, as Mom would put it, when I walked onto the field. Should I go over to Eddie as soon as he arrived and let him know that we *knew* he left the dead squirrel in front of our house for Jeremy, or should I ask him if he did it? I wasn't good at face-to-face confrontations, but I had to do something.

Eddie came by a few minutes later with his father. He helped Mr. Gordon unload the bats and catcher's stuff, then headed straight for me.

"Hey, how're you doing, sport?" He threw one arm around me and waved at Danny.

"Hello, Eddie," I answered, my heart banging away. Maybe Jeremy and I were wrong. Could Eddie actually have *killed* that small animal just because he was mad at my brother?

"Hey, cheer up, Adam," Eddie said, grinning. "Someone would think you've seen a dead ghost." He slapped his hands to his side and broke up laughing. That did it. That was all the proof I needed.

"You think you're so smart, don't you?" I demanded. "Killing a poor squirrel and leaving it for Jeremy."

He shut up real quick. We stared at each other for what seemed like minutes.

"What are you talking about, huh?" He tried to sound outraged but didn't quite make it. I pressed on.

"You know what I'm talking about. Just because you and Jeremy had a fight is no reason to do a sick thing like that."

Eddie looked around. A few of the boys were watching us and his father was coming our way. He lowered his voice in a menacing tone so that only I could hear him.

"You better watch what you say, Krasner. You're as dumb as your brother if you think you can blame me for killing a squirrel and leaving it for Jeremy." He grabbed my arm and squeezed until it hurt. "And if you have any brains in your head you'll know enough to stop spreading lies like that. If you know what's good for you."

I tried to shake his hand away but he was too strong. Before I realized what was happening, Danny had taken a swing at him and jabbed him on the shoulder. Eddie winced and released his grip, ready to hit Danny. But his father reached out and shook Eddie by the neck like a mother cat shaking a baby kitten.

"Fighting again, eh?" he said through clenched teeth. "I'll deal with you later."

Eddie cringed away from his father. Why, he's afraid of him, I realized, wondering why I'd never noticed it before.

"All right," Mr. Gordon shouted to everyone standing in a circle watching what was happening. "Start jogging three times around the bases and home plate starting from here." He pointed to the spot where we stood.

I got in place behind Danny and Eddie stood behind me.

"I won't forget this, Krasner," Eddie muttered.

"Neither will I," I answered, making my voice sound as tough as I could. But in spite of my bravado, I was scared—scared of what Eddie might do next.

CHAPTER
9

*T*hat night Mr. Gordon called to tell me that I'd made the All-Star game.

"Gee, thanks," I told him, tripping over my words. "I'll make you glad that you picked me!" Ick! I could have kicked myself for saying such a dumb thing.

"I'm sure you will, Adam," he answered kindly. "The game's scheduled for next Thursday. At five o'clock at your school field. The play-offs are Monday and Tuesday evening. Hope it doesn't rain, because if it does, everything gets thrown off schedule."

I was all set to say good-bye when Mr. Gordon cleared his throat. "I couldn't help noticing the fracas at practice today. You and Eddie looked pretty angry. I—er, hope you two are still friends."

"Sure we are," I answered quickly.

"Eddie's a good kid," Mr. Gordon said with a forced laugh, the kind adults make when they say something that really isn't true, "but he gets upset too easily. Then he opens his big mouth and tells people off. He's lost enough friends that way. But I know he really likes you, Adam. He's told me so many times."

"Yeah, I know," I said politely. I couldn't bring myself to tell him about the squirrel. "Well, good night, Mr. Gordon."

"Good night, Adam. See you on Saturday."

I hung up wondering about Eddie and his father. That afternoon Eddie was definitely afraid of him. Mr. Gordon was the sergeant type, always serious and tough. I knew he was always hardest on Eddie during practice, but I'd never thought anything of it. Now that I thought about it, Eddie would cringe whenever his father told him to step into the pitch or hold his mitt lower. I wondered if Mr. Gordon expected too much from Eddie, the way Mom sometimes expected too much from Jeremy, thinking he'd be all right with time and tutors. Then I thought of all the bad things Eddie had done and wondered what his father would do if he found out about them.

•   •   •

Saturday's game was the crucial one for us. If we beat the Starlight Delis, it meant that we'd be in fourth place and in next week's play-offs. Our team got to the field early so we'd be warmed up and ready to play our best.

I was pitching to Richie when I heard a girl call out: "Hi, Adam."

Then a familiar laugh.

I looked over to where the other team's parents and friends were gathering and saw Patty waving. I don't know why I was amazed to see her. Kerry, her brother, was the Starlight Delis' catcher. I waved back, then threw a fastball to Richie. It was wide.

"Good luck!" she called out just as Richie yelled to me to watch what I was doing. I felt nervous, yet more determined than ever to pitch well today.

To make a long story short, we lost the game 5–4. We all felt bad but, as Mr. Gordon said afterward, we'd played a good game. I knew I'd pitched well, but the thing I was happiest about was that I didn't let Eddie get to me. When he razzed me for walking two men in a row in the second inning, which I did, and for throwing wild when I was shortstop and he was pitcher—covering first on a play—which I didn't, I just ignored him. Each time he shut up quickly when he saw he couldn't get a rise out of me.

So this is the way to do it, I thought. How did I ever let him get under my skin the other times? I was too busy concentrating on the game to give it much thought, but I knew it had something to do with the fact that before his opinion meant a lot to me and now it didn't. Still, it made me feel kind of sad. Like I'd lost something.

Since it was our last game as a team, we all decided to go for ice cream at Friendly's with our families. Everyone was for the idea. Everyone, that was, but Jeremy.

"I don't want to go," he whined like a five-year-old. "They're not my team and I don't care about them."

"Well, it's my team and I want to go." I turned to Dad, who had left work early to watch my last game. "We can go, can't we?"

"I'm not going," Jeremy insisted. "Take me home first."

Dad tried to cajole him. "Come on, Jeremy. Since when do you turn down an offer of ice cream? I thought you loved the stuff."

"I do, but not when that creep Eddie Gordon goes along."

"But he's part of the team; you know that," Mom said patiently. She still couldn't bring herself to believe that he'd do a thing like that—not a well-brought-up boy who'd been to her house.

"Well, I'm not going," Jeremy screamed at the top of his voice.

"Shut up," I yelled back, ready to hit him. "You ruin every good time for me." Everyone was heading for the parking lot. As usual, I was going to be left out because of my stupid brother.

Dad grabbed my arm to stop me from punching Jeremy. It was then that I noticed Eddie watching us from a distance, grinning. I felt sick.

I ended up going to Friendly's with Danny and his family. Our group took over the whole place. It looked like everyone was having a good time laughing and talking. Not me. I just sat there, feeling awkward and strange. Whenever Jeremy threw one of his tantrums I was forced to own up to the truth—because of him my family was different from everyone else's. You never knew when he'd get upset and carry on. Actually, it didn't happen very often anymore. The trouble was, there was no predicting when it would happen. But when it did and other people were around, I wanted to murder him and disappear at the same time. Being Jeremy's brother was a royal pain in the neck.

. . .

There were only two more weeks of school. We hardly did any work anymore, which was a good thing since none of us could concentrate, with all the great activities coming up: the All-Star game, the play, the class party, and graduation. Now that the sets were finished, Danny and I fell into the habit of watching the play rehearsals after school. We didn't watch, really, but talked with

Patty and Michelle until it was time for them to say their parts on stage. Monday and Tuesday evenings Danny and I went to watch the Little League play-offs. The Lawson Cleaners won, beating the Starlight Delis 7–5 in a very exciting game.

Wednesday afternoon we played softball after school. Eddie was there, too, but it was no problem. We simply avoided each other. Silently, I complimented myself for acting so "maturely," as Mom would say. We both lived in the same neighborhood, didn't we? I couldn't very well tell him to get lost and he couldn't tell me to, either. Once I caught him staring at me, a sneer on his mean little face all covered with freckles. Well, let him, I thought.

After dinner that evening Mom called to Jeremy to come and talk to her and Dad out on the terrace. He walked past me in the den, a funny expression on his face. I turned the TV down low so I could hear what was wrong. Dad was sitting in a lounge chair, looking sad. But Mom was boiling mad. She started lacing it into Jeremy for playing with Tommy Stein, after being told not to so many times. It seemed she happened to turn down Tommy's street and caught them playing out front.

Even from a distance I could see that Jeremy had turned a bright red. "Aw, Mom, I had nothing to do so I went bike riding. Tommy just *happened* to be there so we started playing."

"You shouldn't be out bike riding. You should be home studying for your finals. You know that."

"I did study. With Mrs. Dawson. I just needed a break."

"I distinctly told you *not* to play with Tommy Stein, didn't I? He's much too young for you."

Jeremy stood there with his head hanging. I felt kind of sorry for him. He had no friends besides Tommy. Just his garden and his Beatles records.

"If I find out that you've gone there again, you'll be grounded. For a month." She shot out the last three words like bullets.

Jeremy jerked up his head in surprise. "But Mom, I have—"

"That's enough, Jeremy," Mom broke in sharply. "I don't want to hear another word about that child."

Jeremy nodded. He looked like he was about to cry. Then he walked toward the glass doors. I turned quickly so he'd think I'd been watching TV all this time, but he didn't even notice me as he passed through the den on his way to his room. I braced myself for the bang of his door but none came. Funny. Jeremy *always* slammed his door when he was mad.

The next day, Thursday, the temperature hit the mid-nineties. It was the hottest day of the year so far. The sun was still broiling in the late afternoon when I put on my uniform. I hated having to wear a baseball uniform in 90-degree weather. But it was worth it, to be in the All-Star game, even though I'd found out the day after Mr. Gordon called that the only reason Danny and I were in the game was because both Richie and Jeff couldn't make it. Of course, Eddie and Mark, our team's best players, would be there.

As soon as I got to the school field, Mr. Gordon saw me and handed me a new baseball cap for the game. Proudly, I put it on. Mom and Dad promised to come and watch the game as soon as they got home from work. That was fine with me, since if I ever got to pitch it would be late in the game. I had no idea where Jeremy had disappeared to. I certainly didn't expect him to show up at the game.

It was a different experience playing in the All-Star game. First of all, all the boys on both teams were good players. In fact, I sat out part of the game. But, as it turned out, I got to pitch two innings and managed to get two strikeouts in a row each inning. The crowd cheered, especially Danny and Patty and my parents, who arrived just as I'd started to pitch, so everything was great—as far as I was concerned. Our team lost the game but I didn't care. Just playing in the All-Star game was an experience I'd never forget.

After the game ended, a little after seven o'clock, we went home to get Jeremy and then went out to have dinner at a diner. I just loved walking into the diner in my All-Star cap. The place was pretty full. I spotted a kid wearing an All-Star cap sitting with his family. I hardly knew him, except that his name was Darren and he was in seventh grade.

As soon as we sat down at our booth, Dad started telling me what a great pitcher I was. The waitress brought our menus but he didn't stop praising me. He mentioned the possibility of my going to baseball camp in August. I really ate it up, since Dad didn't usually get this excited, and the idea of getting away for two weeks sounded great, until I noticed Jeremy staring at me. Glaring at me, I should say, with something like hate in his eyes.

"I'm hungry," he announced loudly, "and I'm sick and tired of hearing how wonderful Adam is."

"Let's order," Mom said, trying to be a peacemaker, but Dad got annoyed.

"Wait a minute," he said. "Adam just pitched in an All-Star game and he did a darn good job of it."

Jeremy flung out his hands, almost knocking over his water. "But how many times do you have to say it? It's really very boring, you know," he practically shouted. The man behind us turned to stare at him.

I cringed. Not again, I prayed. Just then the waitress walked over. "Are you folks ready to order?" She seemed to be about college age and had a real smile on her face.

Before Dad had a chance to tell her to come back in a few minutes so he could lecture Jeremy, I spoke up.

"I'll have a cheeseburger and a Coke. And fried onion rings."

Jeremy ordered the same. Then Mom ordered roast chicken, so Dad said he'd have his usual—the fisherman's platter. By the time the waitress left, Dad and Jeremy had cooled down. But instead of leaving things be, Mom had to go ahead and make matters worse.

"Let's get something straight, Jeremy," she said firmly, looking my brother in the eye. "We're proud of Adam for playing well. Just as we're proud of you when you do something well. Like getting a good grade on a test."

"Come on," Jeremy groaned. "When are you going to let up? I told you I studied for that science test. Yesterday with Mrs. Dawson and all afternoon today."

I looked at Jeremy. That didn't sound like him, studying all afternoon, but I didn't make a joke about it, or even mention that he wasn't home when I'd left for the game. From the way he'd been acting these last couple of days, all excitable and irritable, I figured he'd only explode. I glanced at the kid who'd been in the All-Star game with me. He was sitting a few booths away. We could do very nicely without another of Jeremy's outbursts.

He behaved himself for the rest of the meal, although I

was sure he was going to let loose when Dad reprimanded him for smearing tons of ketchup on his hamburger. We were allowed to pick whatever dessert we wanted. I chose blueberry crumb pie with vanilla ice cream. Jeremy got some gooey chocolate cake that kept him happy while he was eating it. Of course Mom and Dad both said no at the same time when he asked for another piece. I sighed as we got back into the car. Eating out with Jeremy wasn't much fun.

The phone was ringing when we walked into the house. Since I was the first one in, I raced into the kitchen and picked up the receiver.

"Adam? It's me. Danny."

Something was wrong.

"Joe, the school custodian, just called me. The sets are ruined."

He wailed out the last word and sobbed for a few minutes before I could get anything else out of him. What could he mean, the sets were ruined? They were in the auditorium, on the stage. I didn't know if anyone bothered to actually lock the auditorium, but people were in and out of it all day. Besides, Joe was there after school.

"Are you sure?" I asked, certain he was mistaken.

"Of course I'm sure. Joe noticed all the lights on on the stage, so he went inside to turn them off. Somebody threw the sets down and spilled red paint all over them. Every one of them." He started wailing again.

I felt sick. All those hours of work. Why, it took Danny days just to draw each of the sets.

"But who would do such a horrible thing?" I asked.

"I don't know," he said, "but just let me get my hands on him. I'll kill him, that's what I'll do."

I hung up, shaken. What would they do about the

play? It was less than a week away. I turned and noticed my parents and Jeremy staring at me.

"What's wrong, Adam?" Mom asked.

"Someone destroyed the sets. Poured red paint on them."

"That's despicable!" Dad exclaimed. Mom put her arm around me.

Jeremy had a little smile on his face. "Those are the breaks of the game," he said. He went upstairs to his room.

I felt like smashing his face in.

CHAPTER

10

I didn't get much sleep that night. I kept rolling around in bed, thinking about the ruined sets. We'd worked so hard on the details, especially on the file cabinets in the third set. Who could have done such a rotten thing? I tried to figure it out by using deduction. Was it Eddie? Even he wouldn't go that far, would he? Of course it could have been some stranger, or any of the kids in the school. Somehow, I couldn't seem to shake the idea that maybe, just maybe, Jeremy did it. Lately he'd been acting real jealous of me. And he was actually happy when I told him that the sets had been destroyed. Not that that was proof of anything.

The next day in school everyone was talking about the ruined sets. Kids from all grades came over to Danny and me to say how sorry they were about what happened. I knew that the teachers were having a conference with our principal, Mr. Vogel, to decide what to do about the play. A few minutes before the end of recess, Danny and I were asked to go to the principal's office. There were about six teachers sitting in a circle and Mr. Vogel. He was a jolly, round man who smoked a pipe. We must have looked scared because he grinned at us and said, "Relax, fellers. We were just talking about the sets and trying to decide what to do." Then he stared at each of us very intently. "I suppose it all depends on what you two say."

Danny and I looked at each other.

"What I mean is," he went on, "and what it comes down to is—do you boys think that you could redo the sets by Wednesday if you had lots and lots of help?"

Danny scratched his head, thinking. "Well," he finally said, "I saved the original drawings, so I suppose I could draw them again."

Mr. Vogel rubbed his hands together. "Splendid, splendid. That's a good beginning, I must say."

"And I could draw one of the sets, if you wouldn't mind," Mrs. Casey offered.

"Sure," Danny said, smiling for the first time that day.

"But who would paint everything?" I asked. It had taken us weeks to do that.

"What if we organized crews?" Mr. Vogel asked.

"But who?" I asked again.

"All of the sixth graders would be willing to help," Mrs. Hammel said. "I'm sure most of them could paint for an hour or two during the weekend. Then we have all day Monday and Tuesday during school."

It wouldn't be easy, I thought, telling each kid what color to use. And we had run out of some colors. And with so many people around, they'd probably get in each other's way. And . . .

Danny must have been reading my thoughts. He elbowed my arm. "It's worth giving it a try," he said softly.

If he was willing to give it his all, who was I to stop it? "Sure, why not?" I said.

Mr. Vogel smiled. "Why don't you go home and get your sketches, Danny? We can start right now."

Danny cleared his throat. "All right, but first I'd like to ask you if you know or have any idea who could have destroyed the sets."

Mr. Vogel stared at him, then at me. His eyes seemed to bore into mine until I felt so uncomfortable that I had to turn away. Finally he spoke:

"We're not sure at this point, although it's safe to say we have a few leads. Of course the incident had to have occurred some time between three o'clock, when school ended, and seven-fifteen, when Joe discovered the mess. Although it couldn't have happened after six, we don't think, because Joe remembers locking all the doors at that time."

He suddenly smiled. "Let's not worry about who the culprit or culprits are right now. The important thing is to get started immediately on the new sets. You've plenty of work ahead of you."

.   .   .

And so we began Operation Sets that afternoon. Danny and Mrs. Casey finished drawing all three sets around three-thirty, and then we organized groups of five kids to paint each set. It got so crowded in the art room that we moved one set into the auditorium. This set up new problems, like someone needing a color paint that was in the other room. Mrs. Casey was a big help, going to the store twice to get some paints we needed and helping Danny and me supervise the three crews.

At five-thirty we called it quits, and it wasn't a minute too soon. My back was aching from bending over. Danny said he couldn't bear to see another paintbrush or he'd scream. We told the kids to come back at ten the next morning, which was Saturday. Then we got Joe and watched him lock the art room and the auditorium. Nothing was going to happen to these new sets!

We were leaving the school building and about to go our separate ways, when Danny stopped and shook his head. "All day I've been wondering and trying to think of who could have destroyed the sets."

"Me, too," I admitted. But I couldn't bring myself to say who I'd been considering.

Just then Eddie sauntered by, grinning. "I hear you two have had a little trouble."

Danny's mouth tightened. "See you tomorrow, Adam," he said as he walked away.

I started going toward my house. Eddie walked beside me. "Cat got your tongue, Adam?"

"Go away, Eddie," I said, disgusted.

"I will," he said, "but first, don't you want me to tell you who spilled the paint all over your sets?"

A shudder ran through my body. "What could you possibly know about it?" I asked. "Why don't you just mind your own business?"

"But I can't mind my own business," he answered snidely. "I know who ruined your sets."

I walked faster, hoping he'd go away. I was scared to hear what he had to say. It was probably all lies. But suddenly it was the most important thing in the world that I find out what he wanted to tell me.

"Yeah?" I said, trying to sound casual. "So who was it? Santa Claus?"

"It was your brother."

"Jeremy?" I shrieked, although I *knew* that was what he'd say. "You're crazy. You're just trying to start trouble as usual."

He grinned slyly. "You don't like hearing that, do you? Well, it's true, anyway."

"You're a liar," I shouted. "Get lost."

"I saw him creeping around the school yesterday. When I went to get water for everyone during the game. Remember?"

I did remember Mr. Gordon sending Eddie into the school to refill the huge thermos he brought to every baseball game. "You *saw* him?" I asked.

"In the hall. Of course he wasn't doing anything that very second. I guess he waited until I left."

I thought a minute. "That doesn't mean anything. Maybe he went into the school to get some water, too."

"Could be, except that he looked guilty when he saw me. And I heard that they found something belonging to Jeremy in the auditorium. A ruler with his name on it."

"How do you know?" I asked, suddenly feeling sick.

"A kid on my block told me. Didn't you know about the ruler?"

He wasn't lying now. I could tell. I felt nauseated with fear and humiliation. I hadn't known about the ruler. And when I'd been in Mr. Vogel's office, he'd never said a word about it. I could feel my ears turning red, just imagining what Mr. Vogel and all those teachers must have been thinking while I was there. But I refused to accept the idea that Jeremy was the one who did it.

"You're just saying that because you're mad at my brother," I yelled at Eddie, ready to punch him. "Because he beat you up in school."

"Come on, Adam," he said, pushing aside my fist. "You know how jealous he is of you. Remember how angry he got about his garden? I mean, he tore up your entire collection of baseball cards, and all the ones I gave you, just 'cause you stepped on one of his plants."

"Four plants," I corrected him. But Eddie was right. Jeremy *was* jealous of me. I'd only begun to realize how jealous the night before in the diner.

Eddie must have seen he'd gotten to me, because he clapped his hand on my shoulder and grinned.

"Don't take it so hard. I mean, what can you expect from a re-tard."

I shrugged his arm away. "Get lost, Gordon. You're nothing but a creep."

"So that's the thanks I get for telling you," he grumbled. "I should have saved my breath."

I walked away without answering. Nerd! It was plain to see that he *enjoyed* telling me it was Jeremy.

When I got home Mom was there. She looked pale and shaken, the way she looked when Grandma died three years before.

"Where's Jeremy?" I asked after I kissed her cheek, something I'd stopped doing lately.

"In his room. We saw Mr. Vogel this afternoon."

"Mr. Vogel?" So it was true? In the back of my mind I'd still hoped that Eddie had been lying about the ruler.

"They found a ruler with Jeremy's name on it in the auditorium near the sets."

"What does Jeremy say?"

Mom sighed deeply, then sank into one of the kitchen chairs. "He claims that he hadn't been in the auditorium, or in the school for that matter, since your spring concert last month."

"But what about the ruler?"

"I lost it. I don't remember when."

I spun around. Jeremy was standing in the kitchen doorway. His eyes were red. I could tell he'd been crying.

"Eddie says he saw you in the school yesterday afternoon," I blurted out.

"Hah!" Jeremy said angrily. "You still believe that good-for-nothing jerk?"

"Jeremy!" Mom exclaimed.

"Well, I'm sick and tired of everyone saying I spilled paint on those sets. I didn't! I didn't!" He looked at me with sad dog eyes. Trusting eyes. "You know I wouldn't do something like that, Adam. Don't you?"

I looked down at the floor. Anywhere but at those eyes, begging me to believe him.

"Well, dammit," he shouted, "it would be nice if my own family believed me."

"Of course we believe you," Mom said soothingly. She looked at me. "Jeremy isn't a liar, Adam. You know that."

I had to turn away from her gaze, too, silently pleading that I believe my brother. I *wanted* to believe him, but I had to know the truth.

"Well, where were you yesterday?" I asked, my voice sounding tougher than I'd meant it to.

"What is this, a trial?" Jeremy asked. "Where were you on the night of the murder," he said in a deep voice, only it wasn't funny at all.

I persisted. "It would help if you could tell us where you were and who saw you. You know what I mean."

"Of course I know what you mean," he snapped. "I'm not *that* dumb. Mr. Vogel asked me the same thing. And I'll tell you what I told him: I was out riding."

"Didn't you see anyone?" Mom asked.

"No one special," he muttered. "I came home, studied alone since Mrs. Dawson came Wednesday instead of yesterday, then I just went riding around until six, six-thirty. Then I came home and waited for you guys to come back from the All-Star game so we could go out and have dinner." He stamped his foot angrily. "I don't care if you believe me or not. I didn't touch those sets and that's that."

Before I could say a word, he ran out of the kitchen and up the stairs to his bedroom. Mom and I both winced when he slammed the door shut—the loudest, I'd swear, since we'd moved into the house.

Mom bit her lip. "Poor Jeremy. He has so much to bear."

"To bear?" Now I was angry. "Look, Mom, you know very well that he can be destructive. Look what he did to my baseball cards."

"I know what he did," she said evenly, "and I know how frustrating he can be. But let me remind you that Jeremy is not deceitful. If he'd done this terrible thing, he would have admitted it to you by now. I think Mr. Vogel understood that. I can't see why you don't, his own brother."

Now that all three of us were angry, I went up to my room to think things over. I tried to put all the facts in logical order, but they kept chasing after one another, canceling each other out. For one thing, I couldn't deny that Jeremy *was* jealous of me. Also, that he was glad that the sets were destroyed when I told him about it last night. Just as he was glad that we'd lost that ball game that time the fly ball landed at his feet.

Okay, I told myself. So he's happy when I fail at something that's important to me. So what does that prove?

That he poured paint over the sets? Of course not. It only proves that he can't stand to see me succeed, probably because he never does. Then it hit me—the horrible truth of how my brother felt about himself. I tried to imagine being Jeremy—not really good at anything except gardening and playing make-believe games with little kids like Tommy.

Little kids. Tommy! I jumped out of my chair, all excited that I'd hit upon something that might be able to prove that Jeremy was telling the truth. Because I'd decided that Mom was right. Jeremy wasn't a liar. Sometimes he'd exaggerate or omit things, but that was only human. And there was only one way to find out if we were right.

Jeremy was blasting his Beatles music so loudly, he didn't hear me come into his room. He was lying facedown on his bed. When I tapped his shoulder he almost leaped to the ceiling.

"Hey, what do you think you're doing?" he shouted above the blaring din.

"Lower that," I yelled. He reached out and turned down the volume.

"Why didn't you tell Mom and Mr. Vogel that you were at Tommy's house yesterday?" I asked.

"Because then she'd punish me and . . ." He stopped, suddenly realizing that he'd given himself away. "I mean, I didn't see Tommy yesterday," he finished lamely.

He *wasn't* good at lying. For some crazy reason at that moment I remembered Eddie's telling me while we were leaving Gino's that his father was planning on making me starting pitcher that day. Hah! Eddie sure had no trouble lying, for whatever crazy reason he did it. In fact, he was good at it. I felt my heart pumping away, the adrenaline

107

coursing through my body. I felt strong. Like I could take on anything or anyone. But first I had to settle everything with my brother.

"This business with the sets is very serious," I told him sternly. "If you don't tell people where you were, they're going to think you were the one who destroyed the sets. Especially since your ruler was found there."

He hung his head. "I know what everyone thinks and I feel bad about it," he mumbled so softly I could hardly hear him. "But you know Mom. She'll be so angry if I tell her where I was yesterday afternoon. And ground me for a month, besides." He looked at me imploringly. "You heard how she carried on the other night, telling me not to go to Tommy's. I felt awful, knowing all the time that I'd be going there the next day."

"What was so important about your seeing Tommy yesterday?" I asked.

"I wasn't exactly going there to play. I mean, we did play, but that wasn't what was important."

"So, what *was* important?" I asked, exasperated.

"Mrs. Stein asked me to watch Tommy yesterday afternoon. She had to go into the city and all the baby-sitters she'd called were busy. She asked me on Wednesday afternoon and I'd said yes. I was able to go over right after school, since Mrs. Dawson couldn't make it Thursday and had come Wednesday, remember? Even after Mom carried on, I didn't want to disappoint her. Especially since she was paying me a dollar fifty an hour." He smiled sadly. "You know how Mom and Dad never let me earn any money because they're afraid I'll do something wrong. Anyway, I had to get Tommy from their neighbor as soon as I got home from school."

I smiled. It was even better than I'd hoped. "So Tommy's neighbor knows exactly what time you came for him?"

"Of course she does," Jeremy said matter-of-factly. "I went over there as soon as I got home and she was rushing off. Didn't even bother have a snack until I got to Tommy's house. I was there until six-thirty."

I thought about everything he'd just told me. "But you told Mom that you just went riding around yesterday."

Jeremy grinned, proud of himself. "That's what I told Mr. Vogel, too. I planned it out yesterday when I rode home from Tommy's. It worked pretty good, don't you think?"

All he could think of was protecting himself from Mom's anger. He still didn't realize that being with Tommy was an alibi for something a lot more serious.

I sat next to my brother, going over everything Eddie had told me this afternoon. He was obviously lying about having seen Jeremy in my school yesterday.

"One thing I don't understand," I said, "is how your ruler got into the auditorium. Are you sure it was yours?"

"It's mine. Mr. Vogel showed it to me." He turned up his palms and shrugged. "I don't know how it got there, either. I only know that I haven't seen it in a few days at least."

I patted his shoulder. "Don't worry about it. There must be an answer to that, too." The incident with Mark and Laura Lee's locker popped into my head. I stood up.

"I have to make some phone calls," I said. "We'll get to the bottom of all this."

"It's Eddie, isn't it?" he asked quietly.

I nodded. "Who else? Now, all we need is some proof."

"I kind of figured it was him. From the way he acted in school, telling everyone I did it. That it was my ruler they found."

"But he couldn't have possibly known that unless he did it, could he?" I said.

"Guess not," Jeremy agreed, smiling. He tugged at my shirt, suddenly anxious again.

"You're not going to tell Mom about going over to Tommy's, are you?"

"Of course not," I said, grinning. "You are, and right now."

Before Jeremy could protest I pulled him to his feet.

"Go now before you chicken out."

I ran out of the room.

CHAPTER

11

After dinner I went into my parents' room and called Mark. Thank God he was home.

"Did you ever notice Eddie touching Jeremy's books or things?" I asked him.

"You mean, like a ruler?"

My mouth fell open. "How—how did you know?"

Mark laughed, but it was a harsh sound. "It just figures. Eddie's been telling people in school that they found your brother's ruler near the sets, and since he was the only one who knew anything about it, I naturally figured he might have had something to do with the ruler being there in the first place."

I sighed. Good old Mark. "No one in our school knew anything about a ruler's being found on the stage. In fact, Eddie was the one who told me about it."

I shivered. Mark confirmed what Jeremy had said. "You mean, Eddie went around all day telling kids that Jeremy ruined the sets?"

"Right."

"Did they believe him?"

"Some did. Some don't believe anything Eddie Gordon says."

"But, it's a lie," I sputtered. "Jeremy didn't go near those sets and he can prove it, too."

"Good for him. What I'd really like is to fix that little creep once and for all. After what he did to me," Mark said angrily.

"But how can we prove it?" I asked miserably. The excitement I'd felt before calling Mark had disappeared, leaving me depressed. I had no way of proving that Eddie ruined the sets and so everyone would still believe that Jeremy did it, no matter what he said. Then I remembered the fight between Eddie and my brother. It was a good enough reason for Eddie to take revenge—making Jeremy look bad and not caring how many people he hurt. He probably meant to hurt me, too, since I took Jeremy's side and I was no longer his friend. I shook my head in amazement. That kid was sick, all right.

Mark's thoughts must have been running alongside mine. "I'm thinking about the day Jeremy and Eddie had that fight," he said slowly. "Eddie left crying. I remember now that he went over to your brother's books. He stood there a minute—I couldn't see what he was doing. Then he pushed the books on the floor."

I asked eagerly, "Do you think he took Jeremy's ruler then?"

"He could have," Mark said. "All I know is that your brother's things went flying all over the cafeteria floor." He thought some more. "You know, I do remember now. Eddie bent down," he said, excited. "He *could* have picked up the ruler then. I bet you he did."

My mind started churning. "I'll go to Eddie's house

and *make* him admit he spilled paint on the sets. I'll tell him some kids saw him pick up Jeremy's ruler the day of the fight. I'll—"

"Be careful, Adam," Mark broke in. "You're no match for Eddie. You could never trick him into saying anything. He's been lying and conning people all his life. I mean, look what he did to Laura Lee and me."

"What did he have against her?" I asked.

Mark laughed that harsh sound again. "I just found out last week. She wouldn't give him the answers to a math test while they were taking the test. He got 57 on it. The only good thing about it all is that his father punished him for failing."

"There must be something we can do!" I exclaimed, exasperated.

"Like what?" Mark asked. "I don't mean to put you down or anything, but I just can't come up with a way you or any one of us could make him admit to these things he's been doing."

I couldn't fall asleep for hours, even though I was dead tired from getting so little sleep the night before. I was all keyed up and dead set on working out a plan of action. Mom and Dad talked about it for hours, after Jeremy had gone downstairs and confessed where he'd been all Thursday afternoon. Dad was all for calling Mr. Gordon and Mom wanted to handle it through the school authorities. But I had no intention of waiting around. I was going to see Eddie Gordon first thing in the morning. And then what? I asked myself. And then what?

At nine-thirty the next morning I pulled on my shorts and a shirt, then rode my bike over to the school to tell Danny that I'd be back to help him as soon as I got finished at Eddie's.

"I knew it was him," he said slowly. "The rotten nerd."

"You, too?" I said, amazed. "That's what Jeremy and Mark both said. Why didn't you say so yesterday?" At least *he* hadn't suspected Jeremy.

"I had no way of proving it, did I?" Danny asked. "It was just a feeling. Hey," he said, grinning, "want me to come with you? Between the two of us we could beat him up good."

I stared at Danny. He wasn't a fighter. Eddie sure brought out the worst in people.

"No thanks. I'm going alone."

"Good luck," he shouted after me, as the first group of kids started coming into the art room. I waved hello and told them I'd be back soon. At least the new sets were being taken care of. That was something to be grateful for.

As I rode to Eddie's house, I saw myself as a knight on a big white stallion vanquishing the villain. I'd make him admit that he'd ruined the sets, killed the squirrel, and sprayed Laura Lee's locker. I was so engrossed in deciding on a suitable punishment that I must have swerved into the middle of the road. A car honked angrily and I got over to the right. Like Mom always said, accidents often happen when you aren't watching what you're doing.

My heart started thumping as soon as I got to Eddie's block.

When I rang Eddie's bell, Mrs. Gordon came to the door and let me in.

"Hello, Adam," she said in a whispery voice.

"Hi. Is Eddie home?" I asked breathlessly.

She didn't seem to notice I was nervous. "He's in his

room," she said. And, without waiting to see what I'd do, she went into the kitchen.

I found Eddie at his desk, thumbing through a textbook. He turned around when he heard me come into his room.

"So look who's here," he said, grinning. "Now I have a good excuse to stop studying for that dumb history test I have on Monday." He gave me a knowing look. "You'll have to worry about finals next year, like all the rest of us."

My eyes darted around his room, where I'd been several times—to his posters plastered to the walls, his pajamas crumpled on the unmade bed, the baseball cards piled neatly on his night table. It looked like any normal kid's room. Even Eddie looked normal. Not like someone who lied and did nasty things that other kids were blamed for.

I took a deep breath.

"Why did you go around telling everyone that Jeremy ruined the sets when you know he didn't?" I was surprised at how calm I sounded.

He smiled apologetically. "Sorry, Adam. I guess I shouldn't have discussed it with so many people," he said, deliberately misunderstanding my question.

"That's not what I mean and you know it!" I snapped. "Jeremy didn't pour paint on those sets. You did!"

He got up so quickly his chair almost toppled over. He jerked his face toward me so that our noses were almost touching. He'd turned a bright red like he always did when he got angry.

"Watch your mouth, Krasner! Don't start blaming me 'cause your brother poured paint on your precious sets."

I was scared he'd hit me. Even though he was no taller than me, he was a year older and stronger. The doorbell rang, distracting me, but I forced myself to think only about what I was going to do next. I'd jumped into a situation I hadn't prepared for, and right now it didn't look like I was coming out ahead.

"Look," I said, putting my hands up and backing up, "you know that Jeremy didn't do it and my parents know it, too. He was baby-sitting for Tommy Stein that whole afternoon."

Eddie just laughed. "That's great. Now you're getting a little kid to lie and say Jeremy was with him all afternoon. What will you come up with next?"

Without thinking, I pushed him and he landed in his chair. "That's not true and you know it. Not everyone goes around lying like you do, Eddie."

Quick as lightning, he reached out a wiry arm and pushed me hard. I stumbled back against the wall, gasping when I realized that Jeremy was standing next to me. He put an arm around me to steady me.

"Are you all right?" he asked. He looked worried.

"I'm okay," I said when I could catch my breath. "What are you doing here?"

"I had a feeling you'd be here. I didn't want you to talk to him alone. I knew he'd try and hurt you. I just knew it."

I watched my brother stride over to Eddie, looking like he was ready to punch him. I was amazed. Really amazed. Jeremy had come here to protect me! A warm feeling that had to be joy and pride and love all mixed together gushed over me.

"Isn't that touching?" Eddie said sarcastically. "Brotherly love. Now if you're finished checking up on each other, you can both leave. I have to study for a final." He turned his back on us and began leafing through his notebook.

"First I want to know why you went around telling everyone in school that I spilled paint on those sets when I didn't."

When Eddie didn't answer, Jeremy tapped him on the shoulder. Eddie spun around, shoving away his hand.

"Keep your lousy hands to yourself," he shouted. "You re-tard."

"Look who's talking," I shouted back. "Killing squirrels, ruining sets, spraying lockers. You have to be pretty sick to do those things, Gordon, pretty sick."

"You better get out of here fast," Eddie said, panting with fury, "or I'll have my father throw you out."

"I'd rather listen to what they have to say."

We all turned, openmouthed. Mr. Gordon was standing in the doorway.

Oh, no, I thought, my heart sinking into my stomach. Now we were in for it. I knew from experience that parents resented being told that their kids did anything bad. And hadn't Mr. Gordon told me on the phone that time that Eddie was really a good kid? I thought of making a break for it, but he blocked my path, arms crossed, his lips one straight line. Even in shorts and a polo shirt, Eddie's father looked more like a sergeant than ever.

"Adam!"

I flinched as his steely gray eyes bore into me.

"I'd appreciate hearing from you exactly why you and Jeremy came to see Eddie."

It was a command. I cleared my throat.

"Well," I began, since there was nothing else I could do, "Eddie's been telling all the kids in school—the junior high—that my brother ruined our sixth-grade sets—the ones Danny Martin and I made for our class play. But he didn't. Ruin the sets. Jeremy didn't, I mean," I finished weakly.

Mr. Gordon shifted his gaze to Eddie. "Is that true? Have you been spreading this story?"

I looked at Eddie. His face had turned white and he kept swallowing as he stared down at his hands.

"I guess I told a few kids that he poured paint on the sets. Which he did," he muttered resentfully.

"That's a lie," Jeremy sputtered. "*You* ruined them."

"Yeah?" Eddie taunted him. "What about your ruler?"

"How did you know that Jeremy's ruler was found in the auditorium?" I asked.

Eddie turned to me. His eyes blinked a few times. "My neighbor told me."

"When?" I persisted.

"When, when?" he mimicked me. "I don't remember when."

"Nobody in our school knew anything about a ruler being found, but Mark said you were telling kids about it all day yesterday," I said quietly.

Eddie looked from Jeremy to me. "You're all just trying to get me in trouble—you two, Mark, and Danny."

"How did you know about the ruler, Edward?" Mr. Gordon asked in a stern voice.

"I guess Doug Fioretti told me," he mumbled so low I could hardly hear him.

"Shall we call him now and find out if he did?" Mr. Gordon said, hardly moving his lips as he spoke. He was trying to control his rage, but I could feel it, all bottled up and ready to explode. I shivered, wishing I was far away from Mr. Gordon, even though I knew he wasn't angry at

me. For the first time I understood Eddie's fear of his father.

Eddie stared at his father without speaking. He seemed to shrink into himself, to grow smaller.

"Well?" Mr. Gordon barked. "We're waiting for your answer, Edward."

Eddie just shook his head and hunched up into his chair.

"Did you have anything to do with the ruler?"

Head down, Eddie nodded.

"With the sets?"

Again he nodded.

"I want you to tell us about it."

"I spilled paint on the sets," Eddie mumbled. He covered his face, but not before I'd seen the tears running down his face.

"We can't hear you," Mr. Gordon said. "Speak up!"

Again I felt the urge to run out of the room, only I was glued to the floor where I stood.

"I spilled paint on the sets," Eddie repeated a bit louder.

"And what about those other things Adam mentioned before? The dead squirrel and the locker business."

Eddie started sobbing.

"Cut that out!"

Eddie got control of himself, then looked up, not caring anymore that we could all see that he was crying. "I found a dead squirrel," he said, sniffling, "and put it on their doorstep because I was mad at Jeremy. And I sprayed Laura Lee's locker, then put the container in Mark's." He huddled up against his desk and started sobbing again, this time quietly.

Mr. Gordon snorted in air, then he turned to Jeremy

and me. "I'll take care of this and notify the proper authorities, you can be sure."

He nodded at each of us, his jaw clamped shut. We were dismissed.

Jeremy and I ran out of the bedroom and down the stairs. I could hear Eddie's sobs growing louder the farther away we got. Poor Eddie, I thought.

. . .

We jumped on our bicycles and pedaled as fast as we could for home. I felt like we'd just escaped from a dragon. As we were about to pass a little park, I motioned to Jeremy to stop. We sat side by side on the grassy hill, neither of us wanting to talk. After a few minutes Jeremy broke the silence.

"That was some ugly scene," he commented.

"Yeah," I agreed. "I thought I'd feel great, finally getting him to admit he'd done all those things. Only I don't. I feel kind of bad."

"Hm." Jeremy put a blade of grass in his mouth and stared ahead at nothing I could see. "I almost feel kind of sorry for the creep," he said.

I nodded, thinking the same thing. Gently, I punched Jeremy's arm. "Thanks for coming by when you did. He was ready to go after me."

"Yeah, just let him try it," Jeremy growled. Then he grinned and did a most unexpected thing—he threw his arm around me.

"And I never got to thank you," he said. "For sticking up for me. If it wasn't for you—"

I was too embarrassed to let him finish. "Cut it out," I said, standing up. "That's what brothers are for. Come on, I have to get back to the sets. Everyone will think

I'm just slacking off while they're working their little tails off."

"I'll come and help you," Jeremy offered.

I stared at him in surprise. Poor Jeremy. He thought I was about to tell him not to come.

"Don't worry," he said quickly. "I won't do anything stupid. I'll just help out where you and Danny need me."

"Great idea!" I said loudly. "You could carry paint from one room to the other. And help us move the sets into the auditorium when we're all finished."

"So what are we waiting for?" Jeremy threw his leg over his bicycle. "The last one to the school is a rotten egg."

I let him get a head start, knowing I could easily beat him if I wanted to. But I wanted him to win this race. As I rode along, enjoying the cool breeze I made as I pedaled, I could feel the smile growing on my face. Maybe, just maybe, there was some hope that Jeremy and I could be friends. Kind of look out for each other and stuff like that. It wouldn't be like my friendship with Danny or like it had been with Eddie. It would be different—not like most brothers, since we weren't like most brothers— but special in its own way.